DANNY ORLIS
AND
MARILYN'S GREAT TRIAL

DANNY ORLIS

AND

MARILYN'S GREAT TRIAL

BERNARD PALMER

Danny Orlis and Marilyn's Great Trial
© 2024 by Bernard Palmer
All rights reserved. First edition 1959.
Second edition 2024.

Cover image: Adobe Firefly
Character illustrations: John Ball
Editor: Charlene Miskimen

Aneko Press *Youth*

www.anekopress.com

Aneko Press, Life Sentence Publishing, and our logos are trademarks of Life Sentence Publishing, Inc.
203 E. Birch Street
P.O. Box 652
Abbotsford, WI 54405

JUVENILE FICTION / Religious / Christian / Action & Adventure

Paperback ISBN: 978-1-62245-988-9

eBook ISBN: 978-1-62245-989-6

10 9 8 7 6 5 4 3 2 1

Available where books are sold

CONTENTS

CHAPTER 1

A SICK FRIEND

It was a chilly, late winter afternoon. The few warm days had chewed at the edges of the drifts that lined the walks and streets at Cedarton, Minnesota, leaving them ragged and crumbling. The long winter's dirt and grime began to show as the snow settled.

Danny Orlis noted this as he and Kay Milburn made their way across the campus of the Cedarton Bible Institute. He was as tall and vigorous as she was dainty, but somehow they seemed to go together. Perhaps it was the tenderness with which he took her arm as they crossed the street. Perhaps it was the confidence they had in one another, the quiet, natural way in which their lives began to merge one with the other.

"I think it's going to snow again," Danny said, glancing up at the clouds in the manner his dad had taught him back home on the Angle.

"I wish it would."

He glanced down at her and smiled. "I thought you were the one who wanted to see the grass green and the tulips blooming," he told her.

"I do." She paused momentarily. "But this time of year the snow gets so dirty and grimy-looking. I'd like to see a little snow to make things white and pretty again."

"That's just the way our lives get," Danny said, more to himself than to Kay, "when we insist on running things ourselves instead of letting Christ have His way."

They went into the Eat Shop and sat down at a booth.

"I know we always think of snow as purity," Kay replied. "But when I think of a Christian's life, I like to compare it to the summertime. That's when things are growing; when they bear fruit."

The waitress came and took their order.

For a time, Danny did not speak.

"I saw Marilyn's mother on the street the other day," Kay said.

He nodded.

Mrs. Forester had been the subject of all their prayers since Marilyn's salvation. Comparatively wealthy and a socialite, if indeed the little town of Cedarton could be said to have society, she had been furious when Marilyn accepted Christ as her Savior. Later her husband, Harold, came to Christ. That crushed her. In one way or another she had tried to lure them away from a close walk with God. Only the spring before, she had gone out to Cedarton Bible Institute, posed as a Christian, heartbroken over a wayward daughter, and convinced them that Marilyn wasn't suitable material. Harold Forester handled that situation sternly when he learned of it. From that moment on Mrs. Forester had seemed to withdraw. To be sure she renewed her efforts to get Marilyn into a liberal church, but there was a change about her – a hard, impenetrable shell.

"I've never seen her look so old," Kay went on softly, her voice filled with concern. "And so– so–" she paused. "Forgive me, Danny. I don't mean this the way it sounds, but today when I saw Mrs. Forester, I couldn't help thinking that she looks really ugly."

He thought for a moment about his own mother. She had worked hard all her life, bitterly hard. Her hands were red and rough, and wrinkles were beginning to seam her face. But she grew more beautiful, more radiant, day by day.

"I'm sure you're right," he said. "Dad always said that no one twenty years old could take credit for how he looks, whether he's handsome or ugly – but by the time he's sixty he's completely responsible. What's in the heart seems to show through, doesn't it?"

She smiled.

"I couldn't help thinking about your mother," she said, "when I saw Mrs. Forester. There's such a difference between them."

"You can say that again."

"I think it's beginning to tell on Marilyn too," Kay continued slowly. "Have you noticed her in the last day or two? She looks so haggard and pale."

"I mentioned it to Chuck this morning on the way from chapel," the Orlis boy told her. "I thought maybe she was sick or something. But he said she hasn't been complaining any."

"It could be worry over her mother, I suppose." There was a lingering doubt in Kay's voice. "I know that she's been asking prayer for her mother at the group prayer meetings we girls have on Tuesday evenings. And the last time she started, she broke down and cried."

The waitress came with their ice cream. Danny did not speak again until she had made out the check and left it.

"I guess we don't know how fortunate we are to have been born into Christian homes," he went on. "Just think, if you or I had been born to a parent like Mrs. Forester, we might never have come to Christ. Or it would have been as hard for us as it is for Marilyn."

"I'm going to talk to her as soon as I get a chance," Kay said. "I know that she's concerned about her mother, but she's going to get herself down if she isn't careful."

Danny would have replied, but he looked up and saw Chuck and Marilyn come in.

"Hi," he called out, waving his hand.

Chuck and Marilyn both saw them and smiled and waved in return.

"How are things going?" Chuck asked. He helped his girlfriend take off her coat.

"Fine as ever," Danny replied. "Or at least they will be after we have that exam tomorrow."

"It's going to be rough."

When Marilyn was seated beside Kay, he scooted into the booth next to Danny.

"How are you, Marilyn?" Kay asked.

She smiled faintly. "All right, I guess."

Something about her tone startled Danny. He looked up quickly. Strange that he had never noticed before, but Marilyn's face was pale and there was something different about her eyes.

"Danny and I were just talking about you," Kay went on. "We both thought that you've been looking ill lately. Are you sure that you feel all right?"

Marilyn paused momentarily. "I really haven't felt as good as I usually do. The last two or three days I've felt so weak and tired much of the time. I think I must be coming down with the flu or something."

Chuck turned to face her.

"You haven't said anything to me about not feeling good," he said pointedly.

She managed a bright smile. "That's because you'd just start fussing at me to go to the nurse or the doctor or the hospital or something," she said. "I'll be all right. In fact, I feel a little better this afternoon."

Kay was watching her intently.

"It seems to me that you look a little paler this afternoon than you did yesterday," she said. "You ought to go and see the nurse. You shouldn't let anything like that go."

"You're trying to get rid of me," the Forester girl countered. "I know."

"If I had known you weren't feeling good, Marilyn," Chuck said, "I'd have seen that you got to the nurse even if I had to call her for you."

"Now, Chuck," she retorted, "I'm all right. I told you that I've just been feeling weak and achy for the past couple of days. If I don't feel better in the morning, I'll call the doctor or go in and see Miss Fredericks." She paused. "But honestly, I do feel better than I did this morning. I'm sure that I'll be all right by tomorrow."

Then she changed the subject.

"What do you have planned for Bible Club tonight?" she asked.

"I was going to have you handle Bible memorization," Danny said, "but Kay can take care of that for you."

"Oh, no!" she answered quickly. "I'll be there. It isn't going to hurt me just to go to Bible Club. I haven't missed a meeting all year."

Danny knew what she was thinking about; why it was that she was so insistent on going. She and Kay had been doing a great deal of work among the high-school girls. They had secured a list from the principal at the school in town and spent their afternoons visiting with one girl after another.

At one fairly poor home she found the girl interested, but shy and reluctant to get out.

"I just moved here," she protested. "I couldn't go. I wouldn't know anybody there."

"It would be a good way to get acquainted with some of them," Marilyn had said. "You'll find the best high-school kids in town at our Bible Club meetings."

The girl eyed her wistfully.

"I'd like to go," she ventured timidly, "but I don't know whether I will or not. I wouldn't know anybody there. Not a soul."

Kay had told Danny later how they had looked about the home and that it definitely wasn't Christian and the chances were the girl didn't know anything at all about Jesus or the Bible or salvation.

"But you would know somebody there," Marilyn had insisted quietly. "I'm going to be there. And you know me."

The girl brightened.

"But I thought it was just for high-school kids," she said. "What would you be doing there?"

"I'm one of the sponsors," Marilyn answered, "and so is Kay. We'll both be there."

"Honest?"

Marilyn Forester smiled down at her.

"You come," she said. "I'll promise to be there."

Danny knew that was what she was thinking about when she said she had to go to Bible Club that night. Kay was aware of it too.

"She'll understand," the Milburn girl said. "I'll make a special point to go to her and explain what happened the minute she comes in. And we'll all see that she gets acquainted with the other kids and feels at home. There's no call for you to go to Bible Club when you're ill."

"I'll be all right," Marilyn said with finality, and changed the subject.

They sat in the booth for another fifteen or twenty minutes, talking and laughing. Finally Chuck and Marilyn got to their feet.

"We'll be seeing you at Bible Club tonight," Marilyn Forester said with a careless wave of her hand.

"It looks as though she'll be there," Chuck said over his shoulder. "When she gets like this I can't do a thing with her." He laughed.

Danny and Kay remained in the booth until after the other two had left the building.

"Did you notice how white she is," Kay said, "and how drawn her face is? Danny, I'm afraid Marilyn is ill."

He glanced at his watch and started to get to his feet.

"We'd better be going, Kay," he said. "We'll have to hurry to get home for dinner and then over to the Garrett house for Bible Club by 7:30."

She let him help with her coat.

"I don't think it's anything for us to get worried about, Kay," he said. "About Marilyn being ill. As she says, she's probably got a touch of the flu. She did seem to brighten up and feel better after we got to talking about something else."

Danny paid the check, and they went outside together. The snow he had predicted was already beginning to fall. The wind was a whisper, and the flakes, soft and airy, drifted about against a slate gray sky. They dropped to cling silently to his jacket and the wool scarf Kay was wearing over her blond hair.

She smiled happily.

"It's hard to believe that anything could possibly be wrong with the world anywhere," she said, "on a night like this."

THE DOCTOR'S VERDICT

At home Ron came into the living room as Danny took off his jacket. "How'd it go today?" the older Orlis boy asked. "All right," Ron said indifferently, "that is, if you can say that school goes all right."

They sat down in the living room.

"All right," Danny said, laughing. "What's the trouble? What happened to sour you on school all of a sudden."

"Not a thing," Ron said decisively. "Not a thing. Only about this time of year I sure get tired of going. I wish we could go back to the Angle tonight and forget that there ever was such a thing as school. That's the way I feel about it."

"You'll change your mind about that," his older brother told him. Danny got to his feet. "You'd better get your studying finished before long, Ron. There's Bible Club tonight, you know."

The younger boy brightened.

"There is?" he echoed. "That's right. You know, I'd forgotten all about it."

"You'll be there, won't you?"

"Me? Oh, sure! I'll be there. I never miss."

"Then you'd better get up to your room and start studying for that test. Just because there's Bible Club tonight is no reason you shouldn't study for your tests."

Ron stared at him incredulously.

"Danny," he said, "how did you know that I had a test coming up first thing in the morning?"

His brother laughed.

"I remember how I used to be when I was in high school," he said. "Every time I had a rough test or assignment, I would get terribly homesick and wish that I could head back to the Angle too."

Ron shook his head.

"I never saw anyone like you," he said. "I'd sure hate to try to pull anything over on you. You know all the tricks."

"Including the one about talking with someone when I should be studying," Danny said. "Now get along with you. And be sure you study. I'll be asking you how you did in that test in a couple of days."

"All right. All right." Ron disappeared, wearily, up the flight of stairs and went into his room.

For some reason Danny couldn't get Marilyn off his mind during dinner. And when he got to the Garrett home, he was surprised to see her there.

"I see you made it after all," he said to her.

"In spite of you and Chuck and Kay," she answered. "But I do feel better now. And I'm sure being here to help with Bible memorization isn't going to hurt me any."

The work the two Bible school girls had done in visitation showed up in the turnout that night. Although they had concentrated on the girls, a number of new guys showed up too. They kept coming in until the living room was jammed and they spilled over into the dining room.

There was a great time of singing led by Danny and Kay. Marilyn conducted the Bible memory time, and Chuck brought a short, informal message.

The girl Marilyn had been concerned about was there. She sat on the front row, and her eyes never left Chuck Martin's face as she listened intently to what he said. When the meeting was over Marilyn Forester went over to talk with her.

"I'm so glad you came," the older girl began.

"So am I." She spoke with a warmth that hadn't been in her voice before. "It was very interesting. I have never heard anything like that. I want to come again."

Marilyn tenderly put her arm about the girl's shoulder.

"And we want you to come again," she said. "In fact we'd like to have you come to Sunday school and church."

"I'll think about it," she said, "it sounds really interesting."

"I'll call you later in the week," Marilyn told her. "If you decide to go to Sunday school with me, Chuck and I will stop by for you."

The younger girl was ecstatic.

"You're the nicest friend a person ever had," she said. And then she put on her coat and was gone.

Chuck stood momentarily beside Marilyn.

"That was great," he said. "Just befriending that poor kid did so much for her."

She said nothing.

He looked at her oddly. "What's the matter, Marilyn?" he asked. "Don't you feel well?"

"I–I think so." There was a pause in her voice, a hesitation that had not been there before.

"Come over here and sit down for a minute."

"I'll be all right, Chuck." She spoke desperately. "All I need to do is get out in the fresh air. It's so warm in here. I felt faint for a moment."

"I don't think it's so warm in here," he retorted. "The kids have all been going out. They've let in an awful blast of cold air."

By this time Kay came over to them.

"Marilyn!" she exclaimed. "You are sick!"

The two of them guided the Forester girl to a chair where she sat down heavily. Danny moved closer.

"I–I'll be all right in a couple of minutes," she said, her voice quavering. "I don't know what came over me. I felt so weak and–and so hot all of a sudden."

"I knew you shouldn't have come," Chuck Martin said, concern in his voice.

"What do you suppose is wrong?" Kay asked of Danny. She spoke softly so that only he could hear.

Mrs. Garrett came into the living room and felt Marilyn's head.

"You might have a little fever, my dear," she said. "And your pulse is fast."

"I thought maybe I was just getting a bad cold," the girl replied, "or maybe the flu."

"That's probably all it is," the woman said. "Do you have a ride home?"

"She shouldn't ride in that old drafty car of mine," Chuck said firmly. "It just about gives a well person pneumonia on a night like this. I'll call your dad, Marilyn. He'll come after you."

"I hate to bother Dad," she said. "He works so hard all the time."

"I'll bet he won't mind being bothered tonight." Chuck started to call.

"I think I'll be all right as soon as I get to bed," Marilyn managed.

"I'm sure you will," Mrs. Garrett assured her.

Ron Orlis stood on the fringe of the little group that had gathered about Marilyn and waited until Mr. Forester arrived to take her home.

"What happened, Chuck?" her father asked softly as he approached.

"I don't know. She seemed to be all right when

we left the house this evening, but she started feeling weak and dizzy after we got here. I think she's running a fever now."

"It's probably the flu. I'll call Dr. Benton and have him meet us at home if he thinks it necessary."

He dialed the doctor's number.

"She doesn't seem to feel too bad," he explained, "but she is weak and seems to be running a fever."

"I think I'd better see her," the doctor told him. "Take her home and I'll meet you there."

He reached the house shortly after Mr. Forester and Chuck got Marilyn home. He took her pulse and temperature and checked her reflexes.

"If I were you," the doctor said when he finished his examination, "I'd keep her in bed and as quiet as possible for a few days. Give her these capsules according to instructions. And if there is a change of any kind, call me at once."

Both Mr. and Mrs. Forester followed the doctor out into the hall.

"What is it, doctor?" they asked, closing the door so that Marilyn could not hear.

"I don't think it's anything to be alarmed about."

"But what is it?"

"It is a little too early to say with any degree of certainty, but on the basis of the examination I made here tonight it is only a case of the flu."

"I'm glad of that," Mr. Forester said. "It worried me a little when she became sick so quickly."

The doctor set down his bag and got into his overcoat.

"She acts very much as though she's got an old-fashioned case of the flu," he repeated. "She should be as good as new in a couple of days. But there is always a chance that this could be the early stages of something that is much more serious. So be sure to keep me informed at all times, day or night."

Mr. and Mrs. Forester stood together in the darkness, their arms about one another.

* * *

At Bible school the following day Danny Orlis and Kay Milburn were standing in the corridor talking when Chuck Martin came hurrying by.

"Where are you going in such a rush?"

"The Foresters just called," Chuck said. His face was ashen and he kept moving toward the door. "Marilyn's much worse this morning. They asked me to come right out."

One of the guys from Bible school drove Chuck Martin to the Forester home. Chuck sat on the edge of the seat and glanced at the speedometer.

"Can't you go any faster?"

"We're going as fast as the speed limit will allow."

"It seems as though we've been on the road for an hour."

The driver glanced at his watch. "It was exactly six minutes ago that we pulled away from the school."

Chuck ran his fingers through his hair.

"I don't know what I'll do if anything happens to her," he said uncertainly. "It was just a week ago today that we talked about getting married when we're out of Bible school."

"We'll all be praying for her," his friend said. "God can restore her to health."

"I know that." He sighed deeply. "I guess I've got to learn to leave her in His hands."

By this time, they had pulled up to the Forester home and Chuck scrambled out of the car.

"Thanks," he said, starting for the front door on the run. "Would you tell Dr. Nielsen what happened and where I am? I didn't have time to see him before I left."

Mr. Forester met Chuck in the living room.

"I'm glad you're here. She's been asking for you."

"How is she?"

Mr. Forester shook his head.

"They won't know definitely until they get her to the hospital. We're flying her to Minneapolis. There we'll get the diagnosis of a specialist."

"What do they think it is?"

"The doctor says she has some symptoms of a serious illness called transverse myelitis. It is a disorder of the spinal cord and can cause long-term problems."

Chuck's head spun.

Mrs. Forester came into the room just then, wringing her hands and whimpering softly.

"My baby!" she moaned. "My poor, poor baby!"

Her face was devoid of make-up and the lines in her face were etched deeper than Chuck had ever seen.

"Oh, Charles," she exclaimed, hurrying over to him and grasping the lapels of his coat with both hands, "did–did Harold tell you?"

Chuck nodded, but he didn't speak. There was nothing to say. He could still hear Mrs. Forester's broken voice as he walked toward Marilyn's room.

"She's so sick. I just can't stand it. Why doesn't Dr. Benton do something?"

"Carrie," Harold Forester said sternly, "you've got to get hold of yourself. We know Dr. Benton is doing all he can. He's taken care of Marilyn since she was a baby. He's vitally concerned about her. But he doesn't have either the equipment or the hospital facilities to take care of her. That's why he suggested that we fly her to Minneapolis."

Chuck stood for another instant outside the door, his head bowed. Then he squared his shoulders and walked briskly into the room.

He smiled at her.

"Hi, honey!" She spoke weakly.

"What's the big idea?" he asked gently, pulling up a chair and sitting down beside the bed. "It was bad enough to get sick. You don't have to overdo it."

"I had to think of some way of getting out of those tests," she told him.

"That's a good one. You with straight A's." He stopped momentarily, trying to ignore the lump that was forming in his throat. "Your parents tell me you're going to Minneapolis."

"That's what Dr. Benton said," she replied. Her voice was small and far away.

For a long moment she said nothing. Then, with great difficulty, she got her hand out of the covers and tightly clasped Chuck's big fingers.

"Oh, Chuck!" Her voice choked. "I'm so sick!"

Chuck gulped hard and turned away quickly, not daring to let her look into his eyes.

"You'll probably be back home before you know it, sweetheart," he said when he could trust himself to speak.

"You never called me that before," Marilyn said.

"Oh, yes, I have," Chuck told her, "lots of times! Only I didn't say it out loud."

Mrs. Forester came bustling in just then. "Maybe you'd better leave now, Charles, and not tire her anymore," she demanded loudly, her voice trembling. "How do you feel now, darling? Are you any better?"

"I'll be all right."

The older woman looked at her watch again. "I can't understand why that ambulance isn't here. Harold, you'll have to call them again."

"Don't mind Mom," Marilyn said softly. "She imagines the very worst."

"You'd better not talk any more. You've got a trip ahead of you."

"I wish you could go to the Cities with us."

"So do I."

"The ambulance is here, Chuck," Mr. Forester said, knocking on the door.

He squeezed Marilyn's hand tenderly. Even they were hot and dry to the touch.

"I'll be praying for you, honey," he told her. "And so will all the kids at school."

She nodded silently.

There was no caress, no word of love, and yet it seemed as though their hearts were fused together. A strange chill settled over Chuck as they wheeled Marilyn out onto the porch and carried her to the ambulance which would take her to the airport. He was still staring after them when Mrs. Forester came up to him.

"Charles," she said, her voice hushed, "I believe God is going to restore Marilyn to health. I have been saying a prayer for her all day. I called Dr. Carpenter, and he assured me that he too would intercede for her."

"Prayer is a powerful source, Mrs. Forester."

"I don't believe I have ever felt the need to really pray before," she said. "I mean really pray. But this time I told Harold that I know God loves us. And if He does, why would He take away the most precious gift He has given to us?"

"I've been praying too," Chuck told her. "And I know the kids at school will also be praying for Marilyn."

Mrs. Forester looked at him pensively.

"I just wanted to tell you that we are putting our

whole trust in the Lord to take care of Marilyn. I know that you think a lot of her, and I thought it might help to keep you from worrying."

Nevertheless, she was dabbing at her eyes as she got into her new coat and hurried down the steps to the ambulance.

* * *

Kay and Danny met Chuck at the door as he came back to the Bible Institute.

"How is she?" asked Danny.

Chuck shook his head.

"The kids have been holding prayer meetings, Chuck," Kay told him. "Some of Marilyn's classes were dismissed, and they have been devoting the whole time to prayer."

"That's right," Danny broke in. "And it seems as though there are two or three gathered together in almost every corner."

"That's wonderful," Chuck answered.

Mr. Forester called him that evening shortly after they arrived in Minneapolis.

"Marilyn stood the trip very well," he said, "and the specialist who examined her was quite encouraged. He said he wouldn't know until he had made some exacting tests, but it looked as though this might be a light case of TM, if she does have it."

"That's great news."

"Mrs. Forester was wondering if you would call Dr. Carpenter and tell him. He asked her to let him know."

Chuck called Danny and Kay and then tried to get in touch with the pastor of Mrs. Forester's church. But Dr. Carpenter was not in, and he wouldn't be available until early the next morning.

Chuck turned, thankfully, to his books. He had scarcely thought of studying since morning when Mr. Forester had called him. He was still at it when the phone rang some two hours later.

"Did I get you out of bed, Chuck?" Harold Forester asked.

Something in his voice struck fear to the very depths of the boy's heart. "What's the matter?"

"I thought I should call you, Chuck," Mr. Forester continued, striving to keep his voice firm and even. "Marilyn has taken a decided turn for the worse."

There was a long silence.

"Paralysis is setting into her legs. It hasn't affected her breathing or arms yet, but it is very severe."

Chuck's world spun and crashed about him.

"What does that mean?"

The silence came again.

"We won't know for hours. Perhaps days."

What he said after that or how he came to hang up the phone, Chuck did not know. Marilyn was ill! Critically ill. He stopped short, staring out the window into the darkness.

Then in anguish he dropped to his knees!

CHAPTER 3

WAITING FOR NEWS

Chuck Martin did not know how long he remained on his knees. Time ceased to exist. He prayed silently, tortuously. Now the words rushed out in a torrent. Now they ceased altogether as he pleaded inwardly, his very heart crying out to God. The clock in the hall downstairs struck eleven. Still he prayed, pleading that Marilyn would be restored to health.

Finally he could pray no more. He got awkwardly to his feet and went to the window, where he stood looking out into the still, moonlit night.

Just a short time before Marilyn had been as well as he was. Happy, carefree, planning to spend her life in the Lord's service. Now – He choked suddenly and turned back to the dresser. He was still the same. Or was he?

Without quite knowing where he was going or why, he put on his jacket and hat and went downstairs and out onto the sidewalk. The wind that had been blowing during the afternoon had died to a whisper. The snow had been melting during the day but was locked in ice for the night, and there were slick patches on the sidewalk where the water had frozen.

It wasn't cold, but he would scarcely have noticed it if it had been. He crossed the intersection and turned toward the main street.

The fresh air began to clear his head.

At a dark corner, where the streetlight had gone out, Chuck stopped and looked up at the stars. It was one of those still, peaceful nights when it seemed as though millions of winking diamonds were mounted in the soft darkness of the sky, just beyond the treetops.

God was still in His Heaven. He still kept the ordered march of the universe, stayed the stars in their places, and kept the moon on its path. Yet the night was suddenly cold and empty, as though the warmth had suddenly stolen silently away.

Why would something like this have to happen to Marilyn? She had been preparing for full-time Christian service. In high school, at the Bible Institute, and at home she had been a consistent testimony. She was needed so desperately.

Why would something like this happen to her? Why? Why? Why? The questions whirled, unanswered, in a thousand forms through his tortured mind.

It was well after midnight when Chuck finally went back to his room and to bed.

He didn't think that he had slept at all, but suddenly when the strident voice of the telephone awakened him, he noticed that it was light outside.

With a start he sat up in bed, fright squeezing with fingers of iron at his heart.

It was about Marilyn! Even before he looked, he knew who it was.

"This is Harold Forester again, Chuck," Marilyn's dad said. His voice sounded tense and desperately tired.

"How–how is she?"

"If anything, she may be a bit weaker, and the paralysis seems to be spreading."

The boy gasped.

"The doctor says that she isn't a great deal worse than she was last night when I called you, but he told us that we are going to have to prepare ourselves for a long wait. It may be days before we know the outcome."

Chuck stood for a moment or two after Mr. Forester hung up. Then he went miserably into the kitchen and tried to eat breakfast.

At the Bible Institute, Dr. Nielsen met him in the corridor and asked if he had heard any more about Marilyn.

"I think we'll turn our devotional period into a prayer meeting for her this morning," the school president said when Chuck told him of the phone calls. "And we'll set aside one of the classrooms upstairs, so that any who wish may go there and pray during the day."

Chuck's face lighted briefly.

"If you think you should go to Minneapolis now, my boy, or even later in the week, I'm sure we can arrange it."

"That would be fine," Chuck answered. Fine? It would be wonderful. Except that he had only $20.00 in his pocket.

"And Chuck," the school official continued, walking down the corridor with the distraught boy, "I suppose you're finding it hard to understand why a thing like this would happen to Marilyn."

"I've thought a lot about it."

"That's something that bothers all of us at one time or another. Marilyn was preparing for full-time service. She is as committed as any student we have in school and has been working diligently for the Lord."

"That's just what I've been thinking. It doesn't seem fair somehow."

"Humanly speaking, it doesn't seem fair," Dr. Nielsen told him gently. "But *we know that all things work together for good to them that love God, to them that are called according to his purpose.* This is one of the things that we have to take on faith, trusting God to work it out; trusting that it is part of His divine plan."

Somehow Chuck felt better after talking with Dr. Nielsen. He attended the devotional period, drawing strength for himself from the prayers of his friends. And twice, during the day, he went up to the open classroom to pray for Marilyn.

The story of Marilyn's illness flashed across Cedarton, as those things do. Ron and Roxie were terribly concerned when they heard it.

"I just can't believe it," Roxie said, her face clouding. "Why, at Bible Club the other night Marilyn seemed as well and happy as anybody there."

Ron nodded.

"Danny said all the kids out at Bible school are praying for her," he said.

"I don't believe I've ever prayed so hard for anyone," Roxie's voice caught tensely, and for a brief second her eyes brimmed. "What I can't understand is why God would let this happen to a person like Marilyn. She's such a wonderful Christian."

Her twin brother shook his head.

"There must be some reason for it," he answered, "but I don't know. It's hard to see how a thing like this could possibly help anyone."

They walked on toward school together.

"I just wonder if God isn't going to raise her up miraculously. We've been praying for the kids at school and haven't been getting much of anywhere when it comes to reaching them." She stopped and grasped Ron's arm, hopefully. "Ron," she exclaimed, "do you suppose that is why He permitted it? Do you?"

"I suppose it could be. But you know what people say about things like that. They say that God doesn't always let us see His purpose in a thing right away. And that sometimes we can make big mistakes by trying to figure it out. That we ought to just trust Him instead."

"But if it isn't something like that, what could the reason be? How could a terrible thing like this be a part of God's plan? I can't understand it."

* * *

Out at the Bible Institute, when the last class of the day was finished, Kay waited for Danny and Chuck.

"Kay's been eating out since the Foresters are gone, and we thought perhaps you'd like to have dinner with us this evening," Danny was saying to Chuck as they approached her in the corridor.

"I don't know. I'd like to. I–I sure don't feel much like being alone. But I need to be sure I am available if Mr. Forester would call."

They went down to the little cafe and took a booth back in one corner where they could be alone. It was early for the regular dinner crowd, so the cafe was almost empty.

The waitress came to take their orders.

It seemed good to Chuck to be able to get his mind off Marilyn's sickness for a few minutes. As they talked about school and spiritual things, he relaxed a little. Now and then he even laughed.

They were just finishing their dessert when the phone rang. Chuck got hurriedly to his feet.

"I–I'll be right back."

He was gone for several minutes. When he returned, his face was pale and his eyes had taken on a bleak, haunted look.

For a moment he stood by the table without speaking. Kay and Danny both stared at him.

"What's the matter, Chuck?"

He was biting his lower lip savagely.

"Was it Mr. Forester?" Danny asked him.

"He thinks I'd better go to Minneapolis right away."

CHAPTER 4

"NO CHANGE"

Chuck Martin stared at Danny and Kay, a strange look on his face.

"Is Marilyn worse?" Kay had to force out the words. She had grown to love Marilyn more than ever since she had been living at the Forester home.

"Her weakness is getting worse. Mr. Forester said that the paralysis has started to affect other parts of her body."

"Oh, that's too bad!" Kay said softly, a lump forming in her throat. "I was so in hopes that she would be better."

"She's asking for me," Chuck said. "And the doctor thought it would be a good idea if I went down right away."

Danny got quickly to his feet. Kay did the same.

"Is there anything we can do, Chuck?"

"I–I don't know. I'll have to get my suitcase, and–" He paused.

"How are you on money?"

"I've got enough to get down to Minneapolis, but I don't know what I'll do about staying or getting back."

"Go home and get your things ready," Danny said. "I'll have some money for you by the time you're ready to go."

"Listen," Chuck protested, "you're having a hard enough time financially without trying to help me."

"Go on," Danny scoffed, "A fine friend I'd be if I couldn't help you when you needed it."

When Chuck was gone Danny turned to Kay.

"I don't have any money either. Would you like to walk over with me to see Mr. Meyer? I think I can borrow some from him."

They went out of the little cafe together and crossed the street.

"Don't you feel terribly sorry for Chuck?" Kay asked. "Marilyn confided in me one evening last week. She told me that they have come to realize they love each other. I think they had planned to be married when they finish Bible school."

Danny nodded. "Poor guy."

"And what about Mrs. Forester? What's all this going to do to her?"

* * *

At the big hospital in Minneapolis, Mrs. Forester paced up and down the corridor.

"You had better come and sit down, Carrie," her husband said gently.

"What time did you say Charles would be here?"

"He was going to take the first bus out. He ought to be here in half an hour or so."

Mrs. Forester sat down silently beside him. She took a tissue from her purse and dabbed at her eyes again.

"Would you care to go down to the bus depot with me?"

"Marilyn might need me," she retorted.

"We ought to be back in thirty minutes. I think it would be good for you to get away for a little while. The doctor is with her."

Mrs. Forester got to her feet mechanically as though she had no mind of her own and allowed him to help her into her coat.

The nurse came out of Marilyn's room and would have hurried past them, but Mrs. Forester grasped her by the arm.

"How is she?"

"There's no change," the nurse answered, as gently as possible. "Ordinarily there is little change in cases like this for hours – sometimes days."

Mrs. Forester did not speak until she and Mr. Forester were out in the car and were headed toward the bus depot.

"Marilyn has been such a good girl, Harold," she said when they were alone. "I just can't understand why a loving God would let a thing like this happen to her. Why would He let it happen, Harold? Why?"

Her husband did not answer. The lines had deepened in his haggard face; and his eyes, usually so alert, reflected the great weariness that had settled over him.

"I've been saying prayers regularly, Harold," Mrs. Forester went on in a dull monotone. "I've promised God that I would do anything if only He'll make Marilyn well." She stopped, choking back the tears. "What's the matter, Harold? Doesn't God care?"

"Of course, He cares. But, Carrie, we can't strike a bargain with God. We can't make a deal with Him for Marilyn's health. We can ask Him to heal her if it's His will. But after that we must leave the matter in His hands."

She bit her lower lip again.

"Harold," she said at last, "if Marilyn doesn't–doesn't get well, I'll never have anything to do with God again!"

Harold Forester put his arm about her shoulder tenderly.

"I'm sure you don't realize what you're saying, Carrie. God is good! We can trust Him with Marilyn, whatever comes."

Although they hadn't seen it, the Cedarton bus had pulled in a few moments before. Chuck saw them in front of the bus depot and came hurrying out.

As he approached, Mrs. Forester began to cry.

Chuck got into the car quickly, and they drove back to the hospital. Marilyn's mother sat with her head buried in her hands, sobbing now and then convulsively. In front of the hospital Mr. Forester turned to Chuck.

"You go in and talk to Marilyn. Carrie and I will be along in two or three minutes."

The special nurse was hovering over Marilyn when Chuck stepped timidly to the door. She came over to him.

"You must be Chuck Martin," she said pleasantly.

"That's right."

"You must be someone very special," she said, smiling. "We've been looking for you, haven't we, Marilyn?"

But the boy scarcely heard her.

"Is–is it all right if I go in?"

"She's in the ICU," the nurse answered. "But I think it would be all right if you stand just inside the doorway."

He looked at all the machines that made Marilyn look even more helpless and tiny than before.

"Here," the nurse said, crisply, "I'll turn you a little, Marilyn, and adjust the mirror. You'll have to see this handsome young man who is here to visit you."

Marilyn smiled weakly.

The nurse motioned for Chuck to move a step or two to the right. Marilyn smiled when she saw him.

"I asked Dad to call for you," she said weakly.

"I wanted to come right away, but didn't know if they'd let me in."

The silence in the little room was heavy. The nurse shuttled back and forth efficiently, checking machines, and going about her duties with reassuring confidence. After a few moments she left the room.

"Chuck," Marilyn said when they were alone together, "why would God let this happen to me?"

His throat constricted suddenly, and he turned away. Mr. and Mrs. Forester came to the door just then and he spoke to them.

Chuck Martin stayed in Minneapolis all the next day and the next. They allowed him to stand in the doorway for a few minutes every morning and afternoon. If there was any change in Marilyn's condition, he couldn't see it.

Two more days passed, and Chuck felt that he had to get back to school.

"It isn't that I don't want to stay here with you, honey. I guess you know that. I'll be here every minute of the time, in my thoughts at least. But I've got to get back to school. And besides–" His voice trailed away.

"Your money is running low, isn't it?"

"I borrowed some from Danny."

"You should have come to Dad."

He shook his head.

"That's one place I shouldn't go," he replied. "But I'm getting along fine."

He stood there staring at her awkwardly, then turned abruptly and left.

He saw her for a moment that evening before going to the bus depot to go back to Cedarton.

"I'll call you every day, Chuck," Harold Forester promised, shaking his hand. "You know we're doing everything we can for her."

Chuck nodded. "And I'll be praying."

Marilyn's mother, who had been sitting in the easy chair in the hotel room, closed the big Bible she had been reading. "You won't forget to pray for our darling, will you, Charles?" she asked, as though she hadn't heard him a moment before.

"People everywhere are praying for her," he said. "Out at the Bible Institute, the faculty and students – everyone – has been asking God to work out His will for her."

"I know she's going to be made well," Mrs. Forester said with grim determination. "I just know it! I've never been so sure of anything in my life."

"Now, Carrie," her husband cautioned.

"But I do know it, Harold. There must be a purpose in all this, as you said. But I know she's going to be completely well. God is a God of love. He wouldn't let a good Christian girl like Marilyn be struck down this way and not raise her up again."

Chuck smiled at her weakly, but with a smile, nevertheless. Mrs. Forester's confidence offered him a ray of hope.

Mrs. Forester smiled in return.

"It's like Dr. Carpenter always says, we've got to think positively. In this case we've got to believe that Marilyn is not only going to be made well, but that the use of her legs will be restored completely. We've got to determine that she's going to get well. We've got to refuse to believe anything else."

Chuck looked at her. She was so sure that Marilyn would be made well. And yet the lump of ice in the pit of his own stomach grew.

CHAPTER 5

"SHE NEEDS YOUR PRAYERS"

Chuck Martin got up early the following morning, and after a phone call to the hospital to learn how Marilyn had spent the night, he took a bus back to Cedarton. "I'll get in touch with you every day," Mr. Forester assured him as they stood together on the street waiting for the bus to leave, "until Marilyn is completely out of danger."

"I'll be anxious to hear from you."

"And, Chuck," the girl's mother put in, "be sure you remember to pray."

"Don't worry, I'll do that all right," he told her firmly.

"And think positively. Don't allow yourself to think that anything can go wrong. We must have faith."

The bus driver came out just then and Chuck followed him into the big, cumbersome vehicle.

"And remember," Mrs. Forester called after him, "Marilyn is going to be all right."

The tall, blond boy sat down beside the window and watched the endless procession of cars and trucks as the bus driver skillfully threaded his way across the town to the highway that led north.

Mr. Forester called him that evening and the evenings after that as he had promised. But there was little or no change in Marilyn's condition.

"They've taken her out of the ICU," he informed Chuck a few days later.

The boy's heart soared. "She's better, then?"

"That's what I asked the doctor, but he said that it only meant that the critical period had passed."

"And how is Mrs. Forester?"

There was a long silence.

"She needs your prayers, Chuck," Mr. Forester said at last.

When Chuck hung up he went back to his room to write to Marilyn. He had been writing every day, with a forced cheerfulness he did not feel. He told her all the small talk from school that he could remember, how the kids asked about her, and what they would do when she returned. He paused, staring thoughtfully out the window. "If she returned," his anguished heart corrected.

* * *

Roxie Orlis had been trying harder than ever to bring some of her friends to the Lord. She invited them to

Bible Club and youth group and was even able to get Carolyn to promise to go to Sunday school with her.

"What do you do over there?" Carolyn asked. "What's so different about it from any other Sunday school?"

"It isn't that it's so different," Roxie told her. "But the gospel is preached at our church, and you'll just love our Sunday school teacher."

Carolyn pressed her lips together thoughtfully.

Carolyn went to Sunday school and liked it.

"It is fun," she said to the young Orlis girl as they stood on the church steps after the Sunday school hour.

"Wouldn't you like to stay for church too?"

Carolyn shook her head.

"I've had enough religion for one day."

"Maybe you can go to Bible Club with me tomor-row night."

"I'll think about it."

There was a friendly tone to her voice that warmed Roxie's heart. That afternoon she told Ron about it.

"That would be something if Carolyn would trust in the Lord. She's almost as popular at school as Claire is. Maybe even more popular among the freshmen and sophomores." He paused for a moment. "Wouldn't that be great if she'd accept Christ too?"

Roxie's face lighted. "You'll pray for her, won't you, Ron?"

* * *

Danny Orlis sent a message to Tim Barton at Crestwood a day or so after Chuck returned from Minneapolis, telling him that Marilyn was ill. Tim's hands began to tremble as he read.

"What's the matter, Tim?" one of his fraternity brothers sang out. "Did your best gal run off with someone?"

He did not answer him.

"It must be worse than that," another retorted. "Maybe she's suing him for breach of promise."

"Lay off, will you?" Tim started up the stairs to his room.

"Whatever's wrong, you'd better get it fixed up, pronto. Spring football practice starts this afternoon."

When Tim entered his room and closed the door, his roommate, Warren Larsen, looked up.

"What's wrong with you? You're as white as a ghost!"

"I got a message from a guy back home," Tim said, sitting down at his desk. "A girl I used to date is very sick."

"I didn't even know that you had a girl back home."

"She's just an awfully good friend."

Tim checked out his football equipment that evening and went through the first practice mechanically.

Marilyn was ill. Perhaps she was dying. But why?

That question hammered endlessly in his head. She had been living an outstanding Christian life. Every letter from her spoke of Christ, pleading with him to put the Lord first in his life, gently urging him to keep himself separated from the world.

And lately she had been writing about preparing for full-time Christian service.

Now, without warning, she had been struck down. Why? Why?

For the first time in months Tim got out his Bible and began to read. In bed he tossed sleeplessly until he heard the hall clock strike two.

* * *

In Cedarton, Chuck was sleepless too.

It was the nights that bothered him the worst. At times during the day he could almost forget about Marilyn's sickness for an hour or two, under the pressure of studies or the laughter of his friends. But the night hours dragged endlessly.

It was then that he thought of her constantly; wondering how she was, trying to peer into the future. It was then that his own spirits ebbed the lowest and his heart ached with pain that knew no healing.

Mr. Forester had come home now and then to look after his business. He kept assuring Chuck that Marilyn was progressing as well as could be expected. As she entered the third week, they began to wean her off some of the medications.

"She's doing better, Chuck," Mr. Forester told him excitedly when he called that night.

"That's wonderful."

"And tomorrow the doctor is going to give her

a complete physical examination. We should know then just how she's coming along. I'll phone you again tomorrow, just as soon as I get the report."

All night long Chuck tossed sleeplessly. Marilyn was getting better. She must be, or they wouldn't have stopped the medications. And yet–

Chuck was up the following day an hour earlier than normal. He had thought he might hear from Mr. Forester by noon. The doctor usually made the rounds in the morning, and Mr. and Mrs. Forester arranged to see him shortly after his visit to Marilyn's room. The call ought to be coming any time. But the day dragged on endlessly.

Chuck went to the office between classes to see if perhaps Mr. Forester had called the school.

"Are you sure there haven't been any calls for me?" he asked.

"Not a thing, the girl at the desk told him.

"I just can't understand it," he said, shaking his head.

"We'll call you, Chuck," the girl told him, "if a call comes."

But the call didn't come that afternoon.

"I can't figure it out, Danny, "he said as they walked down the corridor toward the front entrance after classes that afternoon. "Mr. Forester said that he would phone me as soon as the doctor finished his examination. And I know he was going to see her this morning."

By that time they were outside the building on the front steps.

"Are you going to youth group tonight?" Danny asked him.

"I don't know."

"You'd better go over to church with Kay and me. It'll do you good to get out with the kids for an evening."

It was then that they noticed the green car that was pulled up to the curb a short distance away.

"Why, there's Mr. Forester now!" Chuck exclaimed.

The older man got out of the car as he saw them and stepped around to the sidewalk.

"How's Marilyn?" Chuck asked breathlessly. "I thought you were still in Minneapolis."

There was a strange, haggard look on Harold Forester's face, and his eyes were sunken and veined with red.

"What's the matter?" Chuck asked. "Is Marilyn all right?"

"Get in, Chuck," Mr. Forester said wearily. "I want to talk to you."

It seemed as though all the strength had suddenly gone out of his body.

CHAPTER 6

THE "GREAT TRIAL"

Harold Forester drove silently around the Bible school's administration building and out onto the highway away from town. Chuck, who had been sitting silently beside him, started to speak impulsively. Then he stopped and moistened his lips with the tip of his tongue. "How is Marilyn?"

"I didn't want to tell you over the phone, Chuck. That's why I drove up to Cedarton."

Fear stabbed deeply into Chuck's heart, and icy fingers seemed to squeeze the breath out of him.

"It's her legs. From all evidence, they seem to be paralyzed."

For the moment Chuck said nothing.

"Are they sure?"

"Two specialists examined her this morning," Harold Forester continued. There were no tears in his eyes, but a taut rasping quality had come into his voice, and his hands trembled a little on the steering wheel. "They give little or no hope for her. She may have to spend the rest of her life in a wheelchair."

Chuck swallowed hard and looked quickly away.

"We've had the best medical help available. We've done everything we could for her. I don't understand why, but the Lord must have a purpose in it."

For two or three minutes the boy could not trust himself to speak.

"What about Mrs. Forester? Does she know it yet?"

Harold Forester shook his head. "I haven't known just how to tell her. She's been so sure the past few weeks that God was going to restore Marilyn's health completely. This is going to be a terrible blow to her."

Chuck nodded.

"I thought it might help if you were there when I told her, Chuck. For some reason Carrie has taken to you these past weeks."

Chuck's forehead wrinkled thoughtfully.

"I'll be glad to do what I can."

"I knew you would. I've tried to talk to Carrie, to get her to see that God's will for Marilyn might not be a complete healing. I've tried to explain that He may not do it in our way, or even in our time, but she thinks God will heal her."

"I guess I don't understand it either," Chuck retorted, almost bitterly.

"We don't have to understand, Chuck," Mr. Forester said kindly. "All we have to do is trust." He turned on to the highway in the opposite direction from town. "Carrie says she's trusting in the Lord, but somehow she got the idea that if she just refuses to believe any differently, Marilyn will be restored to health." He sighed deeply. "I don't know what's going to happen to her now when we tell her that things didn't work out her way."

The sun was dropping silently behind the trees. Brilliant slivers of light blended in riotous splendor against the pale gray of the sky as though all were right in the world. Chuck's heart cried out in protest. It would never be right again!

"It isn't any worse for Mrs. Forester than it is for you," Chuck said, his voice thinly edged with bitterness, "or for me."

The older man glanced at him.

"Yes, it is, Chuck! You see, we have the Lord Jesus. She has no one to cling to!"

* * *

The evening after Tim Barton received Danny's message telling of Marilyn's illness, he reported for football practice at the usual time.

He couldn't understand it. Marilyn was good and fine and zealous for the Lord. Why would God allow a thing like that to happen to her?

As he stood in one corner of the dressing room waiting for the other guys to get into their practice jerseys, his mind reviewed the message again.

It wasn't that he was in love with her or anything approaching it. She had never been more than just a good friend. And yet he could not get his mind on anything else.

"Now I want to see you guys come alive," the coach bawled loudly when they were all out on the football field. "This may be spring practice, but it's still important. You're all going to have to get in there and hustle every minute."

He put them through a brief half hour of conditioning and started them jogging around the tracks. Tim went through the motions, but his heart wasn't in it.

It was the same way the second day and the next.

"Barton!" the coach shouted after Tim threw a pass that went eighteen inches over the outstretched fingers of the receiver. "What's the matter with you, anyway? You've been loafing out here, and I don't intend to stand for it. Now get in there and dig!"

When Tim went back to his position his face was crimson.

* * *

Roxie and Ron were both excited with the prospect of the special meetings which were going on at church. The speaker was a pastor from one of the churches in Minneapolis and spoke at convocation in high school the day the meetings opened. Claire Eaton introduced him.

"You know something?" Carolyn said as she and Roxie went back to their homerooms. "I'd like to hear him speak. He sounds as though he'd be interesting."

"Why don't you go with me to church tonight?"

"I'd like to, but I have some studying to do. I don't know whether I'll be able to or not."

"I'll stop by for you at about seven tonight."

Carolyn hadn't said that she would go, and Roxie hadn't been sure, even when she went after her, that she was actually planning to go. However, Carolyn had her coat thrown over a chair, and when Roxie knocked on the door, she was ready to go.

The crowd at the meeting was fairly small, but the message, straight from the speaker's heart, seemed to reach Carolyn's heart. She squirmed uncomfortably as he closed his Bible and gave the invitation. Roxie, standing beside her, prayed earnestly.

But, when the invitation was over, Carolyn was still standing there, resolutely. Her face was ashen, but her mouth was set with grim determination.

"Carolyn," Roxie said softly, "wouldn't you like to talk with Mr. Baird tonight?"

The other girl looked at her coldly.

"Why should I want to talk to him?" Picking up her coat, she started out of the church alone.

Roxie had to run to catch up with her.

The girls did not speak to each other until they were almost a block away from the little church.

"Wasn't that a wonderful message?"

"I think I've heard better," Carolyn said curtly. She tossed her shoulders, as though to show her lack of concern.

"Wouldn't you like to give your heart to the Lord Jesus?" Roxie asked.

Carolyn's eyes narrowed.

"If I did, I'd let you know. I want to have some fun first. I want to enjoy life!"

"But if you accept Christ as your Savior, you'll really be in a position to enjoy life. Once you put your trust in the Lord Jesus and settle the sin question you'll begin to know what it is to be truly happy."

Carolyn turned to face her. "I don't know how you could be happy. You never go to a movie or a dance or have any fun. I'd die. I'd absolutely die if I had to live the way you do."

Roxie hesitated.

"We don't miss the movies. We have many things which we feel are so much better that we don't need things like that. Being a Christian doesn't mean *not doing* a lot of things. God just sends some things that are better to take the place of things we've given up."

Carolyn stared hard at Roxie.

"That can't be true," Carolyn said. "Look at Marilyn. You can't deny that she has been a good Christian. And look what happened to her!"

Roxie did not answer her. She couldn't.

* * *

Mr. Forester had intended to return to Minneapolis that evening. He drove Chuck to his rooming house and let him out to get some clean clothes.

"How long will it take you to get ready?" he asked.

Chuck glanced at his watch. "I can make it by 6:30. Is that soon enough?"

"I've got to go down to the office and take a look at my mail," Mr. Forester answered. "I'll be back here by that time."

Chuck got ready as quickly as he could. He was just closing his suitcase when the phone rang for him. It was Marilyn's dad.

"I'm completely exhausted, Chuck. I think I'll wait until morning if it's all right with you."

Chuck Martin swallowed his disappointment.

He felt he had to get down to Minneapolis to see Marilyn just as quickly as possible! Yet it was a good five- or six-hours' drive. Leaving tonight they couldn't possibly get there soon enough to see her before morning anyway.

"I'll stop by for you at five in the morning," the older man told him.

Chuck had planned to see Danny and Kay that night, but now he called and told them he wouldn't be there. He didn't want to see them. He didn't want to see anybody.

He went back up to his room and dropped dejectedly into the straight-backed chair beside his bed.

Marilyn in a wheelchair! Lively, fun-loving

Marilyn! Marilyn, who had never been able to sit still for five minutes! Marilyn, tied to a wheelchair for the rest of her life!

How could Marilyn serve the Lord when she couldn't even walk? And she had been planning on serving wherever He called her. She had talked of the Kentucky mountain work, Alaska, or Africa, if that was where God had called her.

And of late the two of them had been drawn almost irresistibly together. But how could she serve the Lord as the wife of a missionary or minister? What could she do from a wheelchair?

He buried his head in his hands. It couldn't be! Surely God must have something different for her life. For a brief moment bitterness filled Chuck's heart. He just couldn't understand God's dealings with Marilyn. He couldn't understand it.

CHAPTER 7

A GREAT VICTORY

Mr. Forester and Chuck left early in the morning for Minneapolis. They drove slowly through the darkened streets to the highway that led south. Neither of them spoke until after they left the city limits.

Chuck turned a little to look at Mr. Forester in the dim early morning light. His companion's jaw was set with granite hardness, and there were crow's feet at the corners of his eyes.

"Marilyn's going to be glad to see you, Chuck. She's asked about you every day."

"Does–does she know?"

The girl's father shook his head. "We haven't told her yet." He took a deep breath. "You know, I've often heard and read things like this happening, but I didn't realize it would come so close. I almost feel as though I'm going to wake up and find that it's all been a terrible dream."

Chuck nodded but did not answer. He had that same feeling of unreality, that feeling that this actually wasn't true, that it wasn't Marilyn lying, wasted and helpless, on that hospital bed in Minneapolis.

And yet it was true. Brutally true.

"This is going to be especially hard for Marilyn. She's a person who always had to be up and doing, if it were only moving the furniture around. When she was smaller, I don't think I ever saw her walk when she could run." There was a hollow, expressionless tone to his voice.

He drove on silently, his mind years away.

Chuck squirmed uncomfortably. Strange thoughts began to nibble at the corners of his mind. He loved Marilyn. There was no doubt of that. But what would it be like to be married to a girl who would never walk? Would he be able to fully serve the Lord if he married her?

Miserably he turned toward the window and stared, with unseeing eyes, at the passing landscape.

"I'm worried about Carrie," Harold Forester said at last. "I don't know how she's going to take all of this. She's had about all she can stand for the past few weeks."

"She's turned to her Bible since Marilyn has been in the hospital. Maybe this will be the means of bringing her to Christ."

"She's been reading her Bible all right. But I'm afraid that's as far as she's going. Somehow she got the idea that she can bargain with God. Every time I talk to her she's got something more she's going to do for the Lord if He'll only spare Marilyn."

Chuck took a deep breath and, bowing his head, began to pray silently.

Finally they drove into the city and pulled up in front of the hospital.

Mrs. Forester came running down the corridor to meet them.

"Oh, Harold, I'm so glad you're back!" She threw herself into the comfort of his arms. "I'm so glad you're back."

"Is everything all right?" he asked her.

"I–I don't know. I have the strangest feeling that something is wrong, but I don't know what it is."

Chuck turned quickly away.

For a long minute silence hung heavily about them. Mrs. Forester stared at her husband, fear growing in her eyes.

"Harold, you're keeping something from me. What's wrong?"

He did not answer her.

"You're keeping something from me." She spoke slowly, numbly, as though someone had suddenly stolen the strength from her body. Her knees sagged, imperceptibly, and the lines deepened in her face. In that instant she had grown very old.

Harold Forester moistened his lips and looked desperately toward the boy who was standing beside him.

Mrs. Forester turned also to Chuck.

"Something's wrong, isn't there, Charles?"

"I–" Chuck began. But the words choked off.

"It's Marilyn!" Mrs. Forester said. Her lips clipped the words as though they burned her mouth. "It's Marilyn! I know it! I've had the strangest feeling about her!"

Harold Forester started to speak. A nurse came rustling by in her uniform. He paused and waited until she disappeared into a room at the end of the hall.

"Yes, Carrie," Mr. Forester began reluctantly. He swallowed hard. "Yes. It is Marilyn. The doctor told me about her yesterday. I wanted to tell you then, but I just couldn't. I talked with Chuck last night."

Mrs. Forester's mouth twitched. Her face was gray, but her voice was firm.

"What is it?" she asked. "Her legs?"

"They think there was too much damage, Carrie." His voice was as flat and lifeless as hers. "They've known all along that there was some damage, but they thought she might respond to treatment. She has such determination – such will to live and be all right. But they doubt very much that she'll ever be able to walk again."

Mrs. Forester gasped, but that was all.

Silence hung about them.

Chuck shifted from one foot to the other nervously. It was visiting hours and a young man came down the corridor humming a little tune. For an instant Chuck was furious at him. What right did that guy have to be so happy when his own world crashed in bits about him?

They had expected Mrs. Forester to go to pieces, to cry hysterically, and collapse in the hall. Instead she stood there, dry-eyed and staring.

"Is the doctor sure?"

"They brought a specialist up from Rochester to verify the diagnosis, Carrie," he told her.

"Will she ever be able to walk again?" Mrs. Forester asked.

He shook his head miserably. "I asked the doctors that same question. They said she'll be able to get around with crutches in a year or so, but as things are right now she would probably never be able to walk alone, even with leg braces."

Mrs. Forester moved a step or two toward her husband, then stopped. A strange look came into her eyes.

"I'm beginning to wonder if there really is a God," she snapped. There was a new hardness in her voice.

"Carrie!" Harold protested, shocked by what she said and the sudden violence in her voice. "You don't realize what you're saying!"

"How can there be a God? No one – not even an animal would hurt someone they loved like this. Someone who loved them as much as Marilyn loved God! Maybe that's the answer. Maybe there isn't a God."

"Carrie, don't talk that way!"

"Look what your God has done to me!" Marilyn's mother answered.

"We can't be bitter toward God just because He has seen fit to answer our prayers differently than we wanted them answered."

Mrs. Forester acted as though she hadn't heard a word. "How could a God of love treat me and Marilyn this way? Why, only last week I promised Him I would go to your church if He would just restore Marilyn to health. I promised Him I would give up the theater and cards, and even all my friends – just everything. But what good did it do?"

Harold Forester shook his head miserably. Chuck started to speak but stopped helplessly. What could he say?

"We must go in and tell Marilyn," Mr. Forester said. "I told the doctor we wanted to tell her."

Without protesting, Mrs. Forester allowed him to lead her down the corridor to the little room Marilyn had occupied the past few weeks.

They walked timidly to the door. Marilyn saw them through the open door and smiled brightly.

"Oh, Chuck! I'm so glad you came!" She looked over at her dad and mother and smiled cheerfully.

"Hi, honey!" Chuck tried to smile, but his heart was crying. "You look so happy this morning."

Her smile was radiant. "I've just had the most wonderful time with the Lord," she told him softly.

Chuck pulled up a chair and motioned for Mrs. Forester to sit down.

"I don't think that I have ever felt as close to the Lord as I have this morning," Marilyn continued, her voice hushed. "It seemed as though He was right here in the room talking to me and telling me that He was going to see that I have the strength to face whatever comes."

Mr. Forester cleared his throat uneasily. "Well," he managed, "I guess the Lord knew you would need extra strength today."

Chuck nodded in agreement.

"You see," Mr. Forester continued, his voice breaking just a little, "there's something we must tell you."

Marilyn looked at Chuck, then over at her mother and father. "What is it, Dad?" she asked.

Mrs. Forester took a tissue from her purse and dabbed at her eyes.

Marilyn looked at her father as he spoke to her softly.

"I'm sorry I have to tell you this, honey," Mr. Forester repeated, "but the doctors just told us yesterday that you may not be able to walk again."

Marilyn Forester's eyes were bright, and a slight smile played on the corners of her mouth.

"I know it, Dad," she said simply.

"You know it?" Mr. Forester asked. "I told the doctor I wanted to tell you."

"No one told me," Marilyn continued. "I sensed it several days ago."

"But you've never let on," he answered.

"I've gone all over it with the Lord," she said evenly. "I don't know why He wants me in a– a" For the space of a heartbeat her voice broke, but it was only for an instant. "I don't know why He wants me to be like this," she continued. "But I know this. It is His will."

They all looked at her in amazement.

"I've been praying that He would help me to walk again," Marilyn continued. "And I'm going to try with all the strength and willpower I have to do just that. But if it's His will that I–that I remain like this, then I know the Lord will give me the strength to bear it."

"At first I couldn't understand it, but I searched God's Word until He gave me real inward peace."

Everyone was very quiet as Marilyn spoke. She turned and reached for her Bible. "Here," she said, opening her Bible, "let me read some of the verses the Lord gave me." In a clear voice she read aloud: *"Peace I leave with you, my peace I give unto you: not as the world giveth, give I unto you. Let not your heart be troubled, neither let it be afraid."*

Marilyn Forester turned the pages of her Bible with familiarity. "Let me read another verse. Then you'll know why I'm able to take this. *These things I have spoken unto you, that in me ye might have peace. In the world ye shall have tribulation: but be of good cheer; I have overcome the world.* I got to thinking about Fanny Crosby and others who have had physical setbacks, but who really amounted to something for the Lord, and I knew I could take it too."

For the moment Chuck's eyes grew misty. He took a deep breath.

At that instant he knew that, regardless of what came, he wanted Marilyn as his own. Life with her, even if she were in a wheelchair, would be far happier than it could possibly be with anyone else.

"The doctor has told me that he's going to send up a wheelchair for me tomorrow," she said. The smile came back to her lips.

Chuck Martin felt strangely comforted. His heart still ached, to be sure, but Marilyn's radiance warmed him immeasurably.

"I've never seen anything like it," Chuck said as they all left the room after visiting hours were over. "She's ready to accept a wheelchair for the rest of her life if that's God's will for her."

Harold Forester's eyes lighted briefly.

"That faith of hers!" he said admiringly. "We should have known how this would affect her. Her love for the Lord is bigger than anything that could possibly happen to her."

Although he spoke to his wife and Chuck, his words were a prayer of thanksgiving and praise.

"If she can take it that way, Carrie, we'll have to show the same kind of courage."

Chuck thought he saw tears welling up in the mother's eyes. But, strangely enough, she did not cry.

"That makes it all the worse," Mrs. Forester said numbly. "If God loved her with half the love she has for Him, He would never have allowed a thing like this to happen."

Harold Forester squeezed her arm reassuringly.

"I wish I could explain it to you, Carrie. It isn't that God wants Marilyn to suffer. It isn't that He wants us to be punished or to suffer. But He has a purpose, a plan. Who knows what effect this will have on the people who know Marilyn? She might be able to bring a lot more people to Christ being crippled this way than she could ever bring being well."

"I promised God," Mrs. Forester repeated dully. "I promised Him that I'd do anything if He would just make her able to walk again. But it was no use!" she retorted bitterly.

CHAPTER 8

"SCRAMBLED"

Down in Crestwood, Tim Barton got a message on the way to the locker room to dress for spring football practice. It was another one from Danny.

He went off in one corner and read it.

"I just received a phone call from Chuck," Danny Orlis had written. "He says that the doctors say that Marilyn may never be able to walk again–"

Tim's head swam! Marilyn! Marilyn, so happy and full of life! In a wheelchair!

"But he said that he has never seen anything like the way she's taking it. He has never seen anyone so radiantly happy as she was the morning they went in to talk to her and Mr. Forester told her the awful truth about her legs. She says that she knows that the Lord is with her. And that is all that matters–"

There was more, but Tim couldn't read it.

God meant so much to Marilyn. He had always

meant much to her ever since that time back in high school when she trusted Christ as her Savior.

A sudden thought stabbed him.

If this had to happen to someone, why hadn't it happened to him? He was the one who had drifted away from Christ. He was the one who had left close fellowship with the Lord and had gone seeking after worldly pleasure and fame.

The realization struck him with sledgehammer blows. He turned suddenly to the guy who was standing beside him.

"Tell the coach I'm sorry, but I won't be able to make it for practice tonight."

"He's not going to like it."

"I can't help it," Tim answered shortly. "I've got something else I've got to do." He couldn't go out there and practice. Not when his mind was reeling.

"You know how the coach is about missing practice. You're apt to get kicked off the squad and lose your fancy job. He doesn't allow any goofing off!"

"This is an emergency!"

The coach was coming down the hall as he left the locker room.

"Hey, Barton! Where do you think you're going?"

But Tim acted as though he didn't hear him. He hurried out the door, across the campus, and out to the place where he had parked his car.

He got in and whirled away from the curb.

What had happened to him during the past few

months? He had come to Crestwood determined to get an education and still serve the Lord, anxious to witness to his friends and to show them by his life that following Christ was the most important thing in the world.

Tim Barton drove across town and out into the country on a narrow, winding road that had been the old highway.

His mind was whirling.

How fast he was driving he hadn't noticed. But his foot had grown heavier the farther he drove. The car began to swerve! And suddenly there was the comer, just in front of him!

Tim Barton's heart leaped as he slammed on the brakes and jerked the wheel. The car careened wildly as he fought to keep it on the road. But it was no use. There was a screech of tires, the car lurched and went crashing over the guard rail and over the embankment!

For a split heartbeat, terror seized him and went surging through his being. The car was going to turn over! It couldn't possibly – But no! It slammed into a great clay bank and all was still.

Tim lay there for what must have been a minute or two. Sharp, driving pains ran up his legs. Sweat beaded his forehead. And for an instant his head swam. He groaned weakly and tried to move.

"Are you all right?" a frightened voice demanded just outside the car.

A passing motorist had seen him go plunging off the road and had stopped.

Tim shook his head. "I–I–"

"Here," the stranger tried the door, "let's get you out of there."

The door was sprung and they had to break the glass to get Tim free.

"You are a mighty lucky young man," the man said as he helped Tim up to the road. "When I saw you go off that road, I thought sure you'd be killed."

Tim nodded grimly. He tried to take a step or two, but his ankle wouldn't hold his weight. It throbbed with long, driving slivers of pain that slammed up into his thigh. He leaned heavily on his companion. The man drove Tim to a nearby hospital where X-rays were taken of his ankle.

"Is–is it broken?" he asked the young intern who X-rayed his leg and treated him for shock.

"Scrambled," the youthful doctor retorted with brutal frankness. "To tell you the truth, it looks as though it has been run through a meat chopper."

"I'm supposed to be out for football. We're in spring practice now."

"I don't think you'll be playing any football this spring," the doctor replied, "or any other spring for that matter."

CHAPTER 9

PAYING THE PRICE

Chuck Martin and the Foresters ate lunch together in a little restaurant not far from the hospital. Mrs. Forester walked between them mechanically and sat down in the booth with her husband.

"Marilyn wants to see you this afternoon, Mrs. Forester," Chuck said after they had ordered. "She wants to talk to you about her legs and how she feels about the whole affair."

"I don't dare go in there," Mrs. Forester answered, her voice trembling.

"Carrie," her husband said, "We've got to realize that it may be God's will that Marilyn be– be this way. You know, the Bible tells us that all things work together for good."

Her gaze lowered and she traced a small triangle on the tablecloth with her fork. When she looked up, her face was hard and firm.

"I thought I loved God once, but if He can do this to me–if He can do this to my little girl–" Mrs. Forester didn't finish.

"I'm sure you'd feel differently if you'd just go and talk with Marilyn alone," Chuck said.

Mrs. Forester's words were clipped and bitter.

"I know Marilyn better than anyone. She's always thinking about someone else. She'll try to make me feel good, but I know what's going on in her heart. She can't fool me. She feels the same as I do."

"I think you're wrong this time, Carrie," Mr. Forester said.

She changed the subject abruptly.

"Have you asked for your ring, Charles?" she wanted to know.

"Ask for it? Why would I do that? We're engaged. We're going to be married."

"M-M-Marilyn wouldn't want to hold you to a promise to marry her now," she said, her lips trembling. "She'll insist that you have your freedom."

Chuck bit his lower lip.

"But, Mrs. Forester, I love Marilyn. I'd rather live my life with her, even though she might never be able to walk again, than with any other girl in the world."

Her gaze caught his and held it forcibly.

"You can't mean that."

"But I do."

Mrs. Forester shook her head. "I just can't understand it. I can't understand it at all."

When they got back to the hospital, it was visiting hours for the afternoon. Mr. Forester insisted that his wife see Marilyn alone.

"But I–I just can't face her alone," she protested weakly.

"Now listen, Carrie," he told her. "Marilyn needs our help now more than she's ever needed it before. We can't let her down now. You've got to go in there and tell her that everything's going to be all right."

She held his hand tightly. "You come with me," she pleaded.

Together they walked into Marilyn's room.

"Hello, Mom!" Marilyn said, smiling brightly and holding out her hand. "I've been wondering when you and Dad were going to come today. I've been wanting to talk to you."

Mrs. Forester tried to speak but could not. Mr. Forester got a chair for her, and she sat down beside the bed. Tears filled her eyes.

"Now, Mom," Marilyn said softly, "don't cry. Everything is going to be all right."

"I–I know."

"I know how you feel, Mom," Marilyn continued. That same tender little smile flitted lightly across her lips. "And I felt that way at first. It was all I could do to face you and Dad and Chuck. And at night after you'd all leave, I'd cry until there just weren't tears left."

Mrs. Forester sniffled and for an instant turned away.

"But then I realized that it was actually a sin for me to have such self-pity," the girl went on. "I got out my

Bible and began to read and pray as I've never done before. I've known it all along, but now I've come to realize that God is really watching over me. I've surrendered my whole life to His will. I know that whatever He has for me is the best, and I'm going to be completely happy."

"At your age," her mother protested, "and with all the plans you and Charles had! I–I just can hardly bear the thought of it."

Marilyn's lips trembled for an instant. But her face was still radiant with a look her mother had never seen before.

"If I can serve God better from a wheelchair or on crutches," she said, "that's what I want. I think I've finally learned what Paul meant when he wrote, *For me to live is Christ, and to die is gain.*"

Mrs. Forester swallowed hard and looked beyond her daughter toward the window that opened out over the green lawn.

Mr. and Mrs. Forester left the hospital room, almost on tiptoes. When the door closed behind them, Mrs. Forester turned and faced her husband.

"I never could have believed it, Harold. I never could have believed it."

* * *

At Crestwood they put Tim Barton's leg in a cast the following morning. When they brought him back to his room in the hospital, the football coach was sitting there waiting for him.

"Hello, Tim!" he said coldly. "They tell me you went out and got yourself busted up."

"I guess so," Tim replied. "I'm awfully sorry about spring practice."

"You should have thought of that before you skipped it yesterday," the coach answered. "You know how important those sessions are."

Tim nodded.

"I hear I'm busted up so I won't be able to get out for practice this spring at all," the boy told him miserably.

"That's what the doctor just informed me," the coach continued. "That's why I came up to talk to you."

Something about his manner chilled Tim.

"You realize, of course, that if you'd been out for football last night, this wouldn't have happened."

Tim nodded.

"Even though I can't get out for practice this spring, coach, I'll keep in good shape this summer and be here early in the fall."

The coach cleared his throat. "Well, we've been able to get a transfer from one of the big schools in the Southeast. The boy has the makings of an All-American quarterback. And he's concerned enough about practice to be out for football every day. So we won't be needing you, Tim."

The boy's face blanched.

"W-w-what do you mean?"

"Just this," the coach continued. "I've been talking with the doctor. He tells me that your ankle is in such shape that it's very doubtful whether you'd be much good to us at all next year. It might be that a series of expensive operations would fix you up, but with this new boy coming we aren't going to have to depend on you. So–"

For a moment or two Tim could not speak.

"I–I doubt that I'll even be able to go to school next year unless I'm able to keep my scholarship and my job."

The coach got to his feet. "That's no concern of mine. You should have thought of that yesterday when you walked out on football practice." He picked up his hat. "I told you that as long as you held up your end of things, we'd play ball with you. When you decided against holding up your end, you wrote your own ticket, Tim."

"But I–" he started to protest.

"You have no one to blame for this but yourself." The coach turned and walked out of the hospital and down the corridor.

Tim Barton lay for a long while on his hospital bed, staring up at the ceiling. He was through at Crestwood.

Finished!

His job and his scholarship were gone. He wouldn't even be able to finish out the year. He bit his lower lip and turned toward the wall.

If only he had stayed at home and attended Cedarton Bible Institute. But he had been so sure last fall that he had done the right thing. He had been so contemptuous of Danny. He was going to Crestwood and play football. He was the big shot!

But it was gone! Gone! . . .

A nurse came in with his dinner, but he didn't eat very much.

"Cheer up, Mr. Barton," she said as she returned to take his tray away. "I understand that you're being released in the morning."

He looked strangely at her.

"I'll let you in on a little secret," he said bitterly. "I've been released already. I mean from school."

He had a little money saved, almost enough to pay the hospital bill. That would help some. And with the insurance money from the car, he would be able to pay his bill at the Fraternity house.

The following morning, after the doctor had made his rounds, they gave him a pair of crutches and called a taxi to take him out to the fraternity house.

A bunch of the guys were sitting in the living room gabbing, as they usually did. They looked up as he came hobbling in, but only one or two spoke to him.

A few minutes later the treasurer came to his room. "I understand you're leaving us."

"Just as soon as I get my things packed."

"There's a little matter of a bill here," the other boy answered. "You'll have to clear that up before you leave."

"I don't have the money right now," Tim told him, coloring. Last month he'd borrowed $50.00 from one of the guys without a word. "It took all I could spare to get squared up at the hospital. But I can get it for you when I get a settlement on the car from the insurance company."

The boy sat down beside the desk. "Have you ever looked at that policy on your car?" he asked, grinning.

"No, why?"

"Take a look at it," he replied. "It's made out to Mr. Carter, the guy who gave you the car in the first place. Now that you're leaving Crestwood you won't get a cent of it."

Tim wouldn't believe him until he got the policy out and looked at it for himself. Sure enough. It was made out to Mr. Carter. But it wouldn't have made any difference whether he had wrecked the car or not. The title was even in the garage owner's name.

"I–I–" Tim stammered. "I–I don't know what I will do about my bill here. I suppose I could let you have that new suit I just got or my leather jacket. Either that, or I'll send the money down just as soon as I can get a job back home."

The treasurer got the suit from the closet and examined it critically. "It's just about my size, and you owe us $200.00. Suppose you give the suit to me and throw in the jacket. Then I'll take care of your bill."

"But I just paid $200.00 for that suit and $80.00 for the jacket."

"Well, it's just up to you, but I can tell you this much. If you don't care to let me have that jacket and suit, you'd better get the money to pay up before you leave. We know how to handle deadbeats here."

Tim's mind was reeling as he handed the fraternity treasurer his new suit and jacket and got a receipt. The guy left without thanking him.

Tim stared at the closed door. That bum ankle of his sure had changed everything.

CHAPTER 10

A MOTHER'S ANGUISH

Back at Cedarton, Ron and Roxie sat in the living room of the Meyers' home.

"Isn't it terrible about Marilyn?" Roxie asked.

Ron nodded.

"I sure can't see how she could serve the Lord that way."

"Neither can I. It almost makes me wonder whether it really pays to serve God."

"We can't say that, Roxie. Of course it pays to serve the Lord. It's the only way to live."

"I didn't mean that," she said, thinking how her words must have sounded. "Not really."

There was a short silence.

"I know this, though, Marilyn's being sick has caused some of the kids at school to do a lot of thinking. If we weren't so old-fashioned and if our church wasn't so conservative, I know we could bring a lot of them to Christ."

Ron looked at her.

"What do you mean?"

"The kids are doing a lot of talking. Now that Marilyn is sick, they think that something terrible can happen to them. I just know we'd be able to get through to some of them and bring them to Christ, but they want to have a good time too. If we had some more modern ideas about going to movies and dancing and things like that, we could get the church filled for youth group and Sunday school, and there wouldn't be any homes big enough to hold the Bible Club."

"But we can't give up our convictions," Ron protested. "We've got to try to live the way the Lord wants us to and attract kids because we're different."

"I suppose you're right," Roxie answered, but she spoke without conviction.

* * *

That night the first meeting of the missionary conference at Cedarton Bible Institute was to be held. Danny and Kay had dinner together in the school cafeteria and went for a walk across the campus before the meeting.

"Somehow what has happened to Marilyn has really gotten to me," Danny said after a time. "It makes me realize that we must decide now what God wants us to do. We must be willing to serve Him. We can't afford to waste a minute, or it might be too late."

"I feel the same way. It almost makes me feel I ought to go out on the mission field right now, without even waiting to get prepared. Only I know that isn't right. We've got to prepare ourselves for the Lord's work just as carefully and just as thoroughly as we would for anything else. Perhaps even more so."

Danny bent over and pulled a little tuft of quack-grass from the campus lawn.

"I know you're right about preparation. But there's actually only one thing I really want to do, and that's go back up to the Angle where I can fish and hunt and do all the things I used to do. There's no real evangelical work there, and I hope to open the church for gospel services."

Kay nodded. "I know how you feel," she answered. "But it's not always what we want. The important thing is to seek out God's will for us, and then strive to carry it out in our lives."

* * *

At the hospital in Minneapolis, Mrs. Forester went in to see Marilyn again that evening. She sat beside the bed and held her daughter's hand while the girl talked happily.

"But I just can't see how you can be so happy," Mrs. Forester said.

Marilyn smiled tenderly.

"Sometimes I can't understand it myself."

"I knew it," her mother retorted quickly. "I knew you were just putting on a front for us. That's what I told Harold and Charles. I told them that you couldn't possibly love God when–when He has treated you like this!"

"But, Mom, I do love Him with all my heart. I did feel a little bitter at first. But then I began to read my Bible and pray. God seemed to tell me that this was His plan for me. From that time on I've had real peace. I can truthfully say that I'm more content now than I've ever been in all my life, in spite of this."

"You don't mean it!"

"But I do," she answered. "I put all my trust in the Lord. He knows all about it. He knows what He has for me to do and how He wants me to serve. And if I can serve Him better this way, Mom, then that's what I really want. More than anything else in the world I want to be doing the Lord's will."

Mrs. Forester swallowed the lump in her throat.

"But I don't see how you could serve God in a wheelchair," she said, her voice trembling.

"I don't either," Marilyn replied. "But I'm just trusting the Lord to use me."

She waited for a long while.

"Mom, why don't you put your trust in Him too?"

Mrs. Forester straightened suddenly. The color drained from her cheeks. She started to speak quickly but stopped.

"I must be going." She got to her feet. "Your father told me that I shouldn't stay very long this evening."

"But I want you to stay, Mom."

Nevertheless, Mrs. Forester made her way to the door. "I'll be back to see you in the morning, darling," she said. And with that she hurried down the corridor.

Mrs. Forester and her husband had a long talk that evening in the hotel room.

"I just can't understand Marilyn," Mrs. Forester repeated. "You'd think that she would be bitter and doubt God's love. But no, she says that if this is His will for her then that is what she wants."

"I know that's the way she feels," her husband answered. "That's one thing that makes it so much easier for me. It's like I've been telling you, Carrie. All things work together for good. We can't see just how this could accomplish anything good, but that's because we can't understand God and His ways. We just have to trust the same way Marilyn is doing."

Mrs. Forester's face clouded, but she did not speak.

"You know, Carrie," he went on hesitantly, "I almost hate to say this. And yet I've got to. Perhaps one purpose of this is to bring you to the Lord Jesus."

She turned to face him, her eyes blazing.

"Now don't you go preaching to me, Harold!" Her voice quivered. "I can't stand it!"

CHAPTER 11

A STRONG TESTIMONY

The nurse helped Marilyn Forester into a wheelchair and Chuck pushed her down the long corridor to the ramp that led to the sidewalk.

"It's so wonderful to be outside again, Chuck." They went across the street and up the block to a park that nestled along the shore of one of the city's many lakes.

"Let's stop here for a while. I just want to look out over the water."

Chuck pushed the wheelchair over to a grassy little knoll.

"I brought you a little gift," Chuck told her. He reached into his coat pocket.

"It's this." He opened a small box and showed Marilyn a sparkling diamond ring.

Marilyn gasped. "Oh, Chuck!" she cried. "It's beautiful!" The light went out of her eyes. "But–but I can't accept it."

Fear struck its talons deep into Chuck's heart. "You can't accept it! Why not?"

"You know I love you, Chuck," she began, "but I'd be a hindrance in your work. What if the Lord should call you to the foreign field? You wouldn't be able to follow His leading."

Chuck started to protest but stopped.

"I believe the Lord led us together, Marilyn," he said at last. "And He'll take care of us in the work for which we're best suited together."

There was a long silence.

"I can hardly imagine what life would be like without you," he continued.

"I feel the same way," she answered, "but we must be certain of God's will."

He nodded thoughtfully.

Marilyn smiled at him tenderly, and then held out her hand. Chuck nervously placed the ring on Marilyn's finger. For the moment, time ceased to exist for either of them.

* * *

Ron and Roxie got ready shortly after supper and went to church for the youth group meeting that night.

"Just think!" Ron said eagerly as they walked along the narrow tree-lined street. "In a couple of weeks, we'll be home. I can hardly wait to get back on the Angle and tie into one of those nice big walleyes or a hungry jack fish."

"It sure is going to be good to see Dad and Mom," Roxie added.

"By the way, you're on the discussion panel tonight, aren't you?" he asked.

"And I've decided what I'm going to say too. I've been thinking a lot about it. It's like I've been telling you, we've got to get out and mingle with the kids if we want to bring them to the Lord. We'll have to go to the same sort of places and do the things they do if we're ever going to get next to them."

Ron stopped and looked at her. "Who hatched out that bright idea?" he demanded.

"It's the truth," his sister went on. "I've been talking with a lot of the girls. We're too old-fashioned for them. If we would go to movies and dances and things like that, they'd see that a person could be a Christian and have a lot of fun too. That'll make them want to accept Christ as Savior."

Ron shook his head. "You'd better not tell the group anything like that. Why, that's like trying to keep everybody well by exposing them to smallpox."

He would have argued with her, but he realized that he couldn't convince her anyway.

Roxie hadn't even noticed that Tim Barton was in the meeting until she had finished her talk in the discussion. Ron sat there, squirming, as she spoke, thinking of the Bible verses he was going to read to her when he got home.

But before the moderator had a chance to get to his feet, Tim Barton stood.

"I realize that I'm just visiting," Tim said, leaning on his crutches and hobbling up to the front. "But I've got to say something. Roxie is wrong!"

Every eye in the room was fastened on him.

"I know she thinks this is what is best for the youth group, and I had the same idea when I went down to Crestwood." He took a deep breath.

"I told her brother, Danny, that I could serve the Lord better at the university than I ever could in Bible school or here at home," he said. "I was going to live in the fraternity house with guys who didn't know the Lord and show them by my life that it was really something to be a Christian. But I was just kidding myself. I didn't influence anyone for the Lord."

He paused and looked about the group.

"There were only two or three times that I was able to work up courage to speak to any of them about Christ. And then they looked at me as though I were a little off or something. It wasn't long until I was doing the same things and living just like all the rest of them."

Roxie's face was white and drawn as he spoke.

"Then when I had an accident and got this ankle busted up, I found out what those friends were really like. Not one of them stuck by me. Not a single one!"

He moved over behind the pulpit and leaned heavily on it.

"I can tell you this much. There'll be a lot of pressure put on you to compromise with Satan and the world. But don't let them kid you. The only way your testimony can have any effect on those around you is to keep yourself untouched by the things of the world. To live such a clean life that they'll want to be like you."

When he stopped talking, the little room was very quiet.

* * *

Chuck Martin had brought Marilyn back to the hospital a half hour or so before dinner that evening. Mrs. Forester was waiting for them. She threw her arms around both Chuck and Marilyn when she saw the diamond ring.

"I just wanted to tell you, Marilyn," she said when she and her daughter were alone together, "that I think I'll go back home for a few days. Charles is going to be here for the weekend and there are some things your father and I have to attend to."

"That's all right, Mom. I'll be going home before long myself."

Mrs. Forester dropped wearily to a chair and brushed back her hair nervously.

"Mom," Marilyn said at last, "have you thought any more about accepting the Lord Jesus as your Savior?"

Mrs. Forester was silent.

"You know, it could be– it would be the most wonderful thing in the world if you would only put your trust in the Lord Jesus."

"I did put my trust in the Lord once, Marilyn. I promised God that I'd do anything He wanted me to do if only–if only–" Her voice trailed away.

Marilyn reached out and took hold of her arm.

"We can't bargain with God, Mom. And if this is God's purpose for my life, if I can serve Him better this way, then I want to be willing to spend my life like this."

Mrs. Forester swallowed hard.

"But to think that you and Charles have just become engaged. You were always so happy, so full of life. And now this." Mrs. Forester paused. "I'll tell you this much, I'm so pleased with Charles' actions. There aren't very many young men who would insist on staying by a girl under these circumstances. He certainly has proved himself a man."

Marilyn smiled.

"I think we both feel the same way about him, Mom. Chuck and I are praying to know for certain what God's will is for us."

"What do you mean by that?"

"We were talking about it this afternoon, Mom. Chuck loves me, and I love him. We both know that we would be very happy together even if–if I am to spend the rest of my life in a wheelchair. But we want the Lord to come first in our lives. I–I don't want to be a hindrance to Chuck in his Christian work. I'd give him up before that."

Mrs. Forester stared at her.

"You mean that you and Charles would actually give each other up if–if–" She did not finish her sentence.

Marilyn nodded.

"It was awfully hard to come to a decision like that," she said. "I don't know how I could ever live without Chuck. But we both feel that we should put the Lord first and do what He wants us to do. If He wants us to have each other, that's what we want, and we would be extremely thankful."

There was a long, breathless silence.

Mrs. Forester moistened her dry lips with the tip of her tongue.

"Do you mean," she repeated, "that you actually love the Lord that much?"

"Mom," Marilyn said seriously, "He gave us each other."

Mrs. Forester swallowed hard and dabbed at her eyes.

"Oh, Marilyn!" Her voice was choked. "You've shown me things about loving the Lord and being a Christian that–that I never would have believed if I hadn't been right here with you. I couldn't understand how you could be like–like this and still be happy. And what you've told me just now, I–I can see that you really do love the Lord."

She paused momentarily. Marilyn squeezed her hand.

"I've been a wicked, self-centered person, Marilyn," Mrs. Forester continued brokenly. "I'm so tired of this religion of the mind. My heart needs something."

Marilyn opened her mouth and started to speak, but Mrs. Forester continued talking.

"I've been trying to make myself believe I had something, but I don't have what you and Dad have. And I don't really know how to go about getting it."

Marilyn's eyes grew starry. For a long while she could not speak.

"Oh, Mom!" she almost whispered. "Dad and Chuck and I have been praying for this day. You don't know how I've longed to hear you say this. You've had religion. What you need is the new birth. You need Christ's life in you."

"But how do I get it, Marilyn?" Mrs. Forester asked sincerely.

Slowly and carefully Marilyn explained the way of salvation to her mother.

"First, admit to the Lord that you are a sinner," she began, "The Bible says that *all have sinned*! Then trust Christ to take your sin away. Just believe Him, Mom. That's what I did. He will do the rest for you. He has already done it for you."

Quietly, but contritely, Mrs. Forester knelt beside her daughter's bed and asked Christ to be her personal Savior.

CHAPTER 12

ALL THINGS WORK TOGETHER

Kneeling beside Marilyn's bed, Mrs. Forester sobbed out her confession to the Lord and asked Him to forgive and take away her sin. When she finished, Marilyn prayed softly. When at last they had finished, her mother got uncertainly to her feet. For a long minute neither of them spoke. She looked down at her daughter.

"You know, Mom," Marilyn said, when she could finally speak, "if this paralysis came to me just to bring you to the Lord Jesus, then it has been worth it all."

Mrs. Forester nodded. When she did speak her voice was tense and broken.

"I–I'd better go now and talk to your father. I know how much of a burden I've been to him."

She kissed Marilyn tenderly, then turned and found her way to the door.

Harold Forester's eyes grew misty as Mrs. Forester told him she had just asked Christ to be her Savior.

"I've been fighting it so long, Harold," she confessed, "I hardly know what to say now. But I do want you to know that I really have wanted to be a Christian. I saw how you changed and what a sweet girl Marilyn was when she became a Christian. I even saw the difference in the churches we attended, but I would not listen to you because I didn't want to give up all my friends and my so-called good times. I wanted to run my own life."

She sighed wearily.

"I'm afraid I made things very miserable for both of you."

"We can forget those times, Carrie. The important thing is that you have accepted Christ as your Savior now. Don't worry about how we felt. We understood and just kept on praying."

Mrs. Forester was silent.

"There's only one thing that bothers me, Harold. I–I don't feel any different. Do you suppose I will?"

"Taking Christ into your life as Savior isn't a feeling, Carrie. It's a decision – an act. But as you take your stand for the Lord you'll begin to feel different. Don't worry about that."

Harold Forester took his wife into his arms.

"I've been praying for this day, honey. Marilyn's walking means a great deal to me. I guess you know that. But I know that she would rather you were a Christian than ever take another step. This is what we've been praying for."

Mrs. Forester swallowed hard.

"To think," she said, her voice quivering, "that I was so stubborn that it took something like this to bring me to my senses."

"You should thank God that you have trusted Christ as your Savior, Carrie. That's what I'm doing."

Mr. and Mrs. Forester drove back to Cedarton that evening, and by midafternoon of the following day the story of her conversion had swept across Cedarton.

"I was never so surprised in my life," Danny Orlis said to Mrs. Meyer and the twins as they sat in the living room that evening. "Mrs. Forester came out to the Bible Institute to talk to Dr. Nielsen. I saw her in the hall, and she told me that she had given her heart to Christ."

"Isn't it wonderful!" Mrs. Meyer exclaimed. "I must admit that while I prayed for her, there were times when I thought it was almost hopeless."

Ron pursed his lips thoughtfully.

"Danny, do you suppose that was God's reason for afflicting Marilyn?"

"We can't say for sure why God does or doesn't do something, Ron. But it certainly could be the reason."

"I'll bet Marilyn is happy tonight," Roxie said.

"I'm sure of it."

They were still talking when Mr. Meyer came in.

* * *

The Annual Spring Missionary Conference at Cedarton Bible Institute was in progress. The speaker that morning was engaged in Bible translation work. From the very moment he began to speak, Danny felt a strange stirring inside.

"Our work is slow and difficult," the missionary was saying. "We go in and learn the language of the tribe. With a paid native speaker, we learn how to write down every sound that particular language uses. We create an alphabet, a dictionary, and some easy reading books. Then, while some are teaching the Indians to read and write, we go on with the work of translating the New Testament into their language.

"It's a work that isn't done in a week, a month, or a year. But the work is basic. After the New Testament is translated into the native language and the Indians are taught to read, missionaries have something solid to build on. . . . "

He continued to tell about the workers in the Amazon basin of Peru and Ecuador. Of the new work in Bolivia. Of the successes and failures that the translators have had.

There were other speakers from time to time throughout the day, but Danny went home that night with the missionary's words still ringing in his ears. For a long while he sat alone in the darkness of his room.

He didn't want to go to Mexico or Peru or the Philippine Islands. All he wanted was to go back to the Angle that he loved so much!

To Danny Orlis the missionary conference seemed to drag on endlessly. He sat there, listening to one message after the other. He heard the questions that the various students asked the missionaries. And he cringed within.

"Don't these messages really get your attention, Danny?" one of the boys in his class asked him that afternoon. "It almost makes me feel as though serving the Lord on the mission field is the only thing."

Danny nodded.

It wasn't that he didn't want to serve God. It wasn't that he did not want to be in the Lord's will or that he did not want to do what God wanted him to do, but couldn't he serve the Lord on the Angle? Wasn't there a definite need there too? There were unsaved people there. Plenty of them. There were wandering Indians on the Canadian side of the big lake. Some of them had never heard of the Lord Jesus and His saving grace. Why couldn't he work among them?

Kay was waiting for him at the close of the afternoon session.

"Isn't this a wonderful conference?" she asked him. "And tonight is the dedication service. I have been praying all day that a lot of the kids will dedicate their lives to full-time service."

"That would be fine," Danny said without enthusiasm. His own heart was like ice. A person could serve God somewhere besides on the mission field. Certainly he wouldn't have to give up everything he loved.

They went through the cafeteria line and sat at a little table in one corner of the dining room.

"I talked to Mrs. Forester this morning at breakfast. She is a different person now. She told me that she was planning to visit every one of her old friends to tell them about the change in her life. She has resigned from the bridge club and the country club too. She told them she didn't feel that their aims and purposes were consistent with a Christian testimony."

"It sounds as though she really means business with the Lord, doesn't it?"

The service that evening gripped Danny's heart from the very beginning.

Why did they have to choose such soul-searching songs? Why did the speaker have to choose a message that hammered at him with sledgehammer blows? He sat there, cringing under the force of the service.

Finally it was over. Then the invitation was given.

"I am not going to urge you," the speaker said, his voice charged with emotion. "You know whether you want to dedicate your life to the Lord or not. You know whether He has been speaking to your heart this evening. But I can tell you this much. If He has been talking to you; if He is leading you to Africa or to South America or to your next-door neighbor, you had better yield to Him. It is the only way a Christian can be happy. It is the only way you can have God's first choice in your life." The appeal was followed by prayer.

The instant the missionary finished praying, Kay got to her feet. She looked at Danny for an instant, then whisked past. From all across the auditorium the students came, by ones and twos, until the space before the altar was crowded with them.

"Go forward!" Danny's heart said to him. "God wants you to serve Him on the mission field. He wants you to give up the Angle and prepare yourself for full-time service. That is His first choice for your life."

"But that couldn't be right," Danny argued inwardly. God would not want him on the mission field. The need for a Christian worker up on the Angle was desperate. At the resort, fishermen who did not know Christ came from all over the country. He could be a witness there, just as his dad was. He could bring some of those men to the Lord Jesus. He would probably be able to accomplish a great deal more there than he could in Africa or in South America. And yet – He cringed inwardly. He knew that God was calling him.

By that time the service was over.

* * *

At the Meyers' home, Roxie was in her room studying when Ron approached the door and knocked lightly.

"Who is it?" she asked.

"Claire Eaton," he grinned, pushing open the door. "Just thought I'd come in and smile at you so you could sleep tonight."

"Ron Orlis," Roxie flushed deeply. "If you don't stop that! If you–" Indignation stole the words from her lips. She glared at him.

Ron threw himself across the bed and turned to face her. "Got all your studying done for tomorrow?"

"I don't know whether I'm ever going to get this English finished. If I get through the English exams tomorrow, I won't worry about the others."

"That is a tough one. But I figure that if I can't get by on what I've learned so far, I can't cram it all in tonight."

"I don't know how you hope to get good grades, Ron, the way you study. I don't think you ever open a book, do you?"

"Oh, sure! Just finished. The only thing is that I don't make such a show of it as you do."

"I don't know why brothers have to be so mean."

He grinned at her.

"You sure are pretty when you get angry," he observed. "Your cheeks get red, and the sparks just fly from your eyes."

"You get out and leave me alone, Ron Orlis! I've got a lot of studying to do."

He was silent for two or three minutes.

"Tim certainly has opened my eyes about a lot of things," Roxie said, closing her books. "He talks as though he really knows what he's saying."

"From what Danny says, he does," Ron answered. "And the poor guy is really out now. He lost this whole semester's work, and now he doesn't know where he's going to school next semester, or even if he can go at all. I guess that goes to show what can happen when we compromise with the world and forget all about the Lord.

* * *

Danny and Kay rode to town on the bus that evening after the service. And, for a long while, they sat together on the steps of the house where Kay stayed.

"I suppose you'll be going back to Mexico as soon as school is out."

Kay nodded.

"Your Aunt Mabel is coming up. I think I'll go back with her."

He wanted to ask about the decision she had made that night. He wanted to ask where she had been called and how she had known that was where God wanted her to go. He wondered whether she was really determined about it or whether he might be able to convince her that one could serve the Lord at home as well as on a foreign field. But somehow he couldn't bring himself to mention it. Finally he said good night and walked home through the warming spring air.

Sleep did not come to Danny that night.

Every time he closed his eyes, he could hear the missionary's voice telling of the need in the countries where the translators were working. It had not been a plea for workers. None of the missionaries had begged.

They had merely told the ways in which they were serving God, the opportunities their fields offered. That was the thing that was gripping Danny now.

The following morning he got up earlier than usual and hurried out to school.

"Is the missionary still in his room?" he asked the girl at the desk.

"I think so. He was supposed to catch a train out of here about noon, but I don't believe he has come down yet."

Danny went up to the translator's room and knocked on the door.

"I was just getting my bags packed. I catch the train to Minneapolis at 11:55."

"I wanted to talk with you about your work." The words were torn from him reluctantly, one by one.

"Do you think you might be interested in becoming a translator?"

Danny shook his head.

"No, sir! More than anything else I want to work up on the Angle with Dad and Mom and help them run the resort. I want to fish and hunt the way I used to. But I know that I can't do that."

The man looked at him.

"Why not?"

"Because the Lord has been talking to me through this conference," Danny blurted. "He especially spoke to me through your message. I haven't been able to think of anything else since I heard it. I feel convinced that it is the kind of work God wants me in."

"Won't you sit down?" The missionary walked over and closed the door.

"Our work is different than some. The important needs are in the most backward, primitive places – tribes that have never heard the gospel and do not want to. The work is anything but easy."

"I understand."

"You will have to spend a couple of summers at one of our linguistics schools," he said, "and do B work or better in the course."

"I know. I don't know whether or not I can do that, but with the Lord's help I'd like to try."

The missionary took his hand. "I'm glad for that, Danny," he said. "The work is exacting, but there is a tremendous need. A need so great that it almost makes us wonder whether we'll ever get it done."

Danny smiled broadly. Now that he had made his decision, it seemed as though a great burden had been lifted from his heart and mind.

The man went over to the dresser and picked up a small notebook.

"I had another caller earlier this morning. There's a girl who is very interested in this work too."

"What's her name?"

The missionary thumbed through his notebook. "Let's see, here it is," he said. "Kay Milburn. Do you know her?"

CHAPTER 13

WITNESSING

Danny Orlis and Kay Milburn went to the library together to study for the final exams.

"I hate to think of tomorrow with all those finals coming up," Kay said as they walked along the narrow street. "I'm really worried about those exams, Danny."

"You should be," he told her, grinning. "One B. That's terrible. And only four As. You're going to have to watch those finals, Miss Milburn, or you'll be taking this year over."

"Just the same, I'll be glad when they're finished."

"I will be too," Danny replied, "and I'll be glad when school is out. I've had about all the studying I want for a while."

She was silent as they walked across the street and turned toward the library.

"What's on your mind?" he asked.

"I was just thinking. We've had a wonderful time

at school this year, but it's going to mean much more to me from now on."

He turned to look at her. "What do you mean?"

"I've finally settled how I'm going to serve the Lord," she told him. "I–"

"Don't tell me," he broke in, struggling to keep the smile from his face. "Let me guess."

"I'm not going out under my mom's mission, if that's what you're thinking."

"The answer is written in your eyes. All I've got to do is read it."

"Danny!" Kay protested.

He stared into her eyes. "It's there, all right, but I can't quite make it out. We should have stopped under a streetlight so I could see it better."

"Danny Orlis!"

"There, I can see it now," he continued. "You–you're going to Southern Mexico to help with Bible translations."

A peculiar look came over her face. She took a step back, involuntarily. "How did you know?" she asked.

"I told you. I read it in your eyes."

"You've been talking to that missionary."

"What makes you think so?"

"He's the only one I talked to about it."

Then the smile went out of his face.

"I talked with him too, Kay. I had to get some things settled in my own mind."

"Do you mean that you've been thinking of translating too?" she asked, incredulously.

Danny nodded.

"You know, I've had an awful time in deciding to dedicate my life, Kay. I guess I fought it so much because I've always wanted to go back up on the Angle and live. I kept trying to tell myself that I could serve God there as well as I could anywhere; that I ought to go up among the Indians and the trappers with the gospel."

There was wonderment in Kay's eyes as she stared at him.

"But when I first heard that missionary tell about the work of the Bible translators the other day, I knew right then that that was where God wanted me. You'll never know what peace I've had since I yielded completely to the Lord."

For almost a minute they stood there, looking at one another.

"Oh, Danny," Kay said softly, "I had never dreamed that you would be going out under the same mission or that you'd be going into full-time service at all! I–I thought I was saying goodbye to you when I decided to go to Mexico."

"And I thought that I was saying goodbye to you, Kay," he answered, "until the missionary told me that you had talked to him about their work."

Kay did not speak. And neither did Danny. For a moment they looked at one another. Then, with new understanding, he took her by the arm, and they walked up the street toward the library together.

* * *

It was exam time at the high school too, and Ron and Roxie had been cramming for their tests.

"I think we'd better go home and go over that English together, Roxie," Ron said as they walked down the corridor that afternoon.

"I don't feel much like studying," she said. "I want to go home for the summer in one way. But in another I hate to think of leaving Cedarton. We've had so much fun."

He grinned at her impishly. "It is going to be rough getting along without Claire Eaton."

"Claire Eaton? I don't know why you think he means anything to me!"

"Not much! You just ought to hear yourself when he comes around!" Ron tightened his lips primly and raised his voice to a high falsetto, "Oh, Claire, that 100-yard dash was devastating! Simply devastating! And those beautiful manly waves in your hair! They make you look so–so distinguished–and–"

"Ron Orlis!" she cut in sharply. "You make me so angry!"

Ron laughed and would have answered, but someone came up behind them.

"Hey, wait," the voice called.

"There's 'Prince Charming' now, Roxie," Ron said under his breath. "Do you want me to scram so you can charm him without me around?"

Roxie kicked him viciously on the shin. He yelped with pain.

"Hey!" Claire called again. "Wait, I've got something to tell you."

They stopped and waited for him.

"Let's go to the shop and have some ice cream," Claire said, taking his place between them. "I've really got some news for you."

"What is it?" Roxie asked.

Ron thought she sounded overly impressed and frowned his disgust at her. When Claire wasn't looking, she quickly made a face at her brother.

They went down to the shop and gave their orders to the waitress.

"Now," Ron asked, "what's this all about?"

"You knew that Marilyn's mother came home from Minneapolis a couple of days ago, didn't you?"

The twins nodded.

"Well, the first thing she did was to make the rounds of all her friends to tell them that she had confessed her sin and had trusted Christ as her Savior."

"That's what I heard."

"Well, she was over to our place last night for almost two hours, just talking to Mom. They had the Bible out and everything."

Roxie leaned forward interestedly. "Why, I never thought Mrs. Forester would do anything like that. She was always so proud and everything."

"That's what I thought," Claire said. "But she did

it. And this morning when I was leaving for school, Mom had just called her and asked her to come back." He paused momentarily, his eyes beaming. "I don't usually go home at noon, but I did today, and Mom told me that she had–had trusted Christ as her Savior."

Something caught in Roxie's throat and she dabbed at her eyes.

"And that's not all. When I left to go back to school, Mom and Dad were sitting in the library and she had her Bible on her lap. She was talking to him, and he was actually listening. It's the first time in my life that I ever saw tears in Dad's eyes."

For a long minute none of them could speak.

"Hey!" Ron said at last. "All of this actually took place because Marilyn got sick."

Claire and Roxie both turned to face him. "What do you mean?"

"You know how Marilyn's mother kept fighting the Lord," Ron answered. "She wasn't going to get any fanatical ideas like Marilyn and Mr. Forester. I just wonder if she ever would have accepted the Lord Jesus if Marilyn hadn't become ill?"

"Do you know what she told Mom?" Claire broke in. "She said she knows that she would never have become a Christian if Marilyn hadn't gotten sick. She said it wasn't so much the sickness but the way Marilyn took it. The girl had such peace in her heart about spending the rest of her life in a wheelchair and was so radiant and content that Mrs. Forester realized for the first time what it really meant to be a Christian."

"It's just as Danny told us," Ron said, "we can't always see what causes God to permit certain things to happen, but we know that *all things work together for good to them that love God.*

"I've been praying and praying and praying for my parents," Claire put in. "And it got so that I couldn't even talk to them about Christ. It didn't look as though they were ever going to come through. And now Mom is saved, and she's got Dad listening while she talks to him. It's the most wonderful thing that ever happened in our house."

"And to think," Ron said, "that we couldn't understand why God permitted Marilyn to get sick."

THE DANNY ORLIS SERIES

The Danny Orlis series, by Bernard Palmer, delivers a blend of adventure, mystery, and suspense through various settings—from the Canadian wilderness to Guatemalan jungles. Danny Orlis, an adept outdoorsman, skilled athlete, and committed Christian, employs his quick thinking, calm bravery, and biblical solutions to confront everyday problems and hair-raising dangers. Early stories focus on Danny navigating school life, sports, and outdoor challenges, while in later books, Danny and his wife Kay provide wisdom and guidance to youngsters facing lifelike situations and challenges. Having sold over two million copies, this series has made Palmer a renowned author in Christian youth literature. Palmer is also the author of the Felicia Cartright series and various other series for Christian youth.

www.ingramcontent.com/pod-product-compliance
Lightning Source LLC
Chambersburg PA
CBHW070659100726
47907CB00007B/2274